Parabolic Dishes

For Robert Pinsky
A great poet
and
a great
guy

Joe Kronsman
MFA
[Meddler
in
Fine Arts)

Parabolic Dishes

parables & short stories on art, love, death and the search for meaning

JOSEPH KRAUSMAN

Parabolic Dishes

Book design by The Troy Book Makers
Printed in the United States of America
The Troy Book Makers • Troy, New York • thetroybookmakers.com

To order additional copies of this title,
contact your favorite local bookstore
or visit www.shoptbmbooks.com

ISBN: 978-1-61468-719-1

Contents

Introduction

PARABLES ARE SHORT STORIES ABOUT LIFE, LOVE, ART, AND A SEARCH FOR MEANING. About half a century ago I got my MFA at University of Massachusetts, Amherst. I hadn't published my MFA thesis called *Parabolic Dishes*. Why publish it now? Well, I believe there may be some joy in it for some. Also, at my age I can't wait much longer. The hoofed stranger may soon be knocking at my door to take me to a place where I'd rather not go.

I've added three stories recently written to the book: "Dognose Rubin," "The Man Who Only Read Jews," and "Mona Levy."

Why the title *Parabolic Dishes*? When I was in the Army, the parabolic dish sent electric impulses in code, transmitted to a receiver. Parabolic comes from parable, a story transmitted, usually on a page, that transmits metaphorical information from one person to another. I start the project with parables, and then short stories.

The master of the parable was Franz Kafka. His main character is Joseph K., a man who was waiting at a door, not being able to cross over. My name is also Joseph K. Perhaps I am waiting for Godot, and I won't make it to the Promised Land.

Maybe we'll make the best of the time being, smile and find and give joy, before the inevitable final hour.

The Man Who Drew Clocks

THE ARTIST ONLY DREW CLOCKS. He was, as it is said, putting in time. His masterpiece was called *Noon*. It was a large, gold clock with a lion on each side. The hands were shaped like human hands, and they came together in prayer at twelve.

His worst painting was called *Time and Tide*. It was a picture of a sea of clocks and a land of time. Since it was difficult to color a land of time, he left the land blank.

One day, a woman came to the artist's shop, as it is written: "To buy her time."

"Oh, that masterpiece of time called *Noon*, I want it very much. How much does it cost? Time can not be very expensive," she said.

"No, my good woman," said the artist, "time is free, but a masterpiece of time is priceless."

"But I'll pay anything for a masterpiece of time."

"What could you give me? You have nothing I want. Could you give me money? Well, that evaporates in time. Could you give me yourself? Well I don't want it. Since I am an artist of time, my fee must be something that goes beyond time. And you, woman, do not possess that which is above time."

"If I can't have *Noon*, how about *Time and Tide?*"

"Oh, you don't want that. It is a failure."

"But I must make some use of time. I must buy something whether or not it is good or bad."

"That is very true," said the artist, " you can have *Time and Tide* for three cents."

Since the woman could not afford a masterpiece of time, she bought a failure, but it too, cost her dearly.

Every Dog Has Its Day

THEY SAY "EVERY DOG HAS HIS DAY." Well I want to tell you about a bitch I once knew. I happen to be a beagle myself, so I'm pretty familiar with dogs. I'm not owed by anyone. Once I had a master who served me canned dog food. Can you imagine me – Herman Fine- eating cheap cereal? "Stand up and beg!" my master said. Sheet. I'm a free dog. I kiss no one's ass. I bit my master on the leg and split. I was out on my own and I enjoyed it. I ran into a scraggy bitch of a spaniel called Mary. She was pretty, but very thin. I liked her. We went through lots of garbage together, runs in the moonlight, barking at mailmen, chasing cats.

But for all the good times I had with Mary, there was always something sad about her. She was never really happy. One day, I said to her, "Mary what gives with you? Don't you care for our scene?"

"Woof," was all she said. If the dogs you are traveling with aren't having fun, the scene is a bummer. "Come on, Mary, tell me what gives?" I asked her again.

She began with her sad tale.

"I was born with a good pedigree. I used to live with a rich family. Although my master was high class, he used to beat me all the time with a stick. He was anti-dog. My back was always sore. If I wouldn't stand when he wanted me to, whack! If I wouldn't sit when he wanted, WHACK! I couldn't take the beatings so I knocked over a few lamps and pissed on the rug. He kicked me out."

"The street was no picnic either. Although my master was a bastard, I ate regular and I had a place to sleep. I ran into some pretty mean dogs on the street. Every passing hound would hop on my back and stick his pecker into me, be he a sloppy mutt, schnauzer, dane, a poodle or anyone else. And what did I get from all my troubles? A few bones, water from the gutter, a show in my head. I never complained. But lately, I got this pain in my side and it's been killing me. I keep my mouth shut. But it ain't no Christmas party. In fact, I never really had a good time 'til I met you, Herman. You sure are one swell dog. But this pain ain't no picnic; that's the reason I ain't walkin' around thinkin' this world is a party."

"Don't worry," I said, "the pain will go away." I tried to cheer Mary up, but it was no good. It got to the point where she couldn't chase cats. She didn't feel like eating anymore. Just to look at her sad eyes could break your heart. What could I do? I'm a pretty smart dog, but I ain't no doctor. I got the best garbage I could find. But it was no use, she didn't want to make love anymore. Then she couldn't run around at all. We lived in a pile of junk on a vacant lot. It was cold. She shivered every night. I told her jokes,, but she wouldn't laugh.

Then the most remarkable thing happened; her bark turned into a whimper, and instead of sounding like a dog, she sounded like a sick cat. The great "Woof, Woof!" turned into a yow…ow…owo. You could hardly hear it. I knew her days were numbered. What can I say? What was her life? Dirty garbage. Where did she live? In a dump. Why was she hungry? Because the rich treat us like dirty dogs. Mary died for the whole working class.

And they say, "Every dog has its day." But I know at least one dog that didn't. No, sir, she sure didn't.

Sorrow's Monk

IT WAS THE CUSTOM OF CERTAIN RELIGIOUS SECTS to bring great pain to themselves; in so doing they believed that they would relieve themselves of the tremendous burdens of Sin Original and Sin Synthetic.

Once a monk hired a flogger to beat him with a whip. Each flog was pain intermixed with joy, for the monk thought that pain in this life would be insignificant compared with what he could possibly get in the next. The flogging was allowed through the grace of the omnipotent deity who created man tainted with sin, but allowed eternal bliss through the proper ceremonies.

This same monk had a servant who cut him with razors on Wednesdays. The monk's back was a mess of blood, hideous scabs, abrasions, and many things we could all do without. The ascetic slept on a bed of stone and walked barefoot in summer and winter.

One Wednesday when the monk was having his back cut in the public square, a singing gypsy strolled by. The gypsy wore long silver earrings and had sideburns with curly hair. He carried a guitar around one shoulder and a flask of wine around his waist.

The gypsy looked in amazement; he could not believe his eyes. Why a man would hurt himself, he could not comprehend. The gypsy was in a good mood, so he started to sing a few gay ditties. The solemnity of the cutting ceremony was disturbed by the singing of the gypsy. The monk was angry. "What are you singing about? The world deserves no song," the monk said. "Repent now, brother; repent before it is too late, before you burn in the lake of fire."

"Don't sweat old man," the gypsy said, "I don't believe in the next world, In fact I don't even believe in this one."

"Insolent vagabond, don't disgrace the holiness of the cutting."

"But your monkhood, would you not rather sing a song with me? I know a good one—it is called "A Benefit in the Haystack."

"Seize him! Seize him!" yelled the monk. And the crowd grabbed the gypsy.

"You deserve a taste of damnation, insolent wretch," the monk said. "I'll give you a taste of hell! Take his shirt off! Let his back feel the sting of the whip; it is only one one-thousandth of the pain he shall feel for eternity."

"Oh," yelled the gypsy, "I was only joking, your monkhood. I would not profane the ceremonies. Please let me suffer in the next world. It would be much worse there. If I am a sinner, don't punish me now. Let me amass a woeful record here, so I can burn in peace there."

"Shut your mouth, dog," the monk said. "Sixteen lashes." And the gypsy was thoroughly beaten.

"What do you think," the monk asked, "of the taste of hell?"

"Let me go! I won't interrupt your ceremonies anymore. Forgive this poor sinner." The gypsy was cut down. And the monk was put on the whipping rack. The gypsy quickly recovered from his pains and strolled over to the hiding place of the miller's daughter. He strolled away singing a lewd, happy song. How difficult it is for gypsies to understand the meaning of symbols. They learn so little from examples, and the monk yelled hideous sounds into the night.

At the Firehouse

THE DOG PISSES ON THE HOSE. Someone across the street from the firehouse buys onion rolls. Some fireman are asleep in bed. It is a lazy day in May. A few buds have just broken open. All traces of snow have disappeared. Four men are playing cards. The alarm sounds. The peace is broken. One player has three kings. He is angry. They ride off in the fire truck to a small house at the other end of town. They see no smoke. Is it a false alarm?

They break the door down. Firemen break the door even if they have a key. It is their way. Inside the house is an old man smoking a pipe.

"Where's the fire?" asks the chief.

"It's in here burning!" the old man yells, as he points to his heart.

"Oh," says the chief, "if we put out THAT fire, your house would fall down."

"But I'm on fire!"

"You mean to tell me you messed up on a good card game just to tell me that? Well so is everyone else."

"I don't give a hoot about everyone else. It's your civic duty to help."

The chief is so impressed with the old man's social consciousness that the giant hose is turned on the old one. His pipe goes out, but he stays on.

"Is this a way to treat an old man?" asks the soggy codger.

"Enough lip," says the chief, "you're just a false alarm. Into the truck boys, and back to the game." They speed off with bells ringing and sirens screaming. The old man stands there wet and dripping; his pipe is out, and his ? still burning.

Tale of a Ski Lodge Worker

I AM WORKING AS A WAITER AT THE SKI LODGE. It is winter and a beautiful blanket of snow has covered the earth.

The snow has come with a message: "I want you to use me properly, trample me with skis and love. The footprint of fulfillment I crave, for soon spring will come and I will melt into nothingness."

I would not have given the snow any attention, for who can believe in talking snow, but a bluebird came to my window and verified the snow.

"Listen, Waiter," the bluebird said, "the snow may melt today. You must go to the ski-master and attempt to fulfill the snow this very day." I who never skied must master the snow. Yet I do not have skis, or boots, or two sharp poles. So I go up to the ski-master who lives on ski-mountain.

"Sir," I say, "I want to rent ski equipment and use the snow for soon it will be spring."

"Aren't you 'L' a waiter at the lodge?"

"Yes, I am."

"Don't you know the staff of the lodge is forbidden to ski here; only guests may ski. Don't you see the sign: These Facilities For Guests Only, No Staff Permitted?"

"But I'm willing to pay for the skis."

"It is absolutely forbidden. If the owner of the ski lodge should discover I let the staff ski, I would be fired. Imagine a worker skiing. Oh, it's too funny for words."

The ski-master breaks into an hysterical laughing fit, so I run away. I was thinking of sneaking out to the mountain at night, on a borrowed pair of skis. But it is not possible. I would be spotted against the pure white snow. It is easy to see a man alone on the mountain at night. Immediately they would know that it was I who broke the rule of the lodge: THOU SHALT NOT SKI. I would be fired. Oh, that would be terrible! For I belong to the lodge, and nothing else.

But I can control myself no longer. I must ski, for soon it will be spring. I go out to the sparkling mountain at night. The sweet, cold crystals have captured my reason, the pure white snow will lead me to death.

An Ape Seder

THIS APE FAMILY LIVED IN THE AFRICAN JUNGLE. They climbed trees, ate bananas, swung from vines and had a heck of a time. There was the momma ape, poppa ape and a young child ape. They were Jewish. The family name was Freedman. Anyhow, this family always went to their favorite watering hole for drinks. Now, on the way to the watering hole they always avoided a certain cave. For in that cave lived a very dangerous animal indeed. In that cave lived none other than the leopard called Harvey Gross!

As you know, leopards eat apes. Being totally eaten results in death, which is usually fatal. So the Freedmans were right in avoiding Gross. Of course, if a leopard is full, you can walk right next to it, and not be eaten. But you never really know if it's full. So why ask?

Since they were Jewish, the Freedmans were obligated to celebrate the Passover. The seder (known to gentiles as The Lord's Supper) is the chief service of the Passover. Momma ape really dusted the tree hut for the seder. Poppa ape made palm wine and jungle matzo. Junior prepared to ask the four questions. The apes were busy and happy. The Freedmans like all good Jews were expecting the Messiah to come soon and for the first time. Oh joyous day.

Anyhow, the night of the seder came. The candles in the tree hut were lit, the table was set, red and green jungle birds chanted beneath the star-lit April sky. All was calm, all was bright.

Junior asked the four questions without making even one mistake. The Passover meal was delicious. Then the part of the service where a cup of wine is poured for Elijah the prophet. A cup is filled with palm wine by the leader of the seder. Everyone rises, and the door is opened for Elijah. Poppa rose with the cup of Elijah. Junior opened the door for the prophet. Poppa recited:

"Pour out thy wrath on the heathen who knows thee not..." And when Poppa was reciting, who the heck do you think charged in the door? Was it Elijah? Nope. Was it a monkey's uncle? No. Was it a donkey's cousin? Nosiree. Was it the Messiah in person? Not by your life; it was Harvey Gross!!

Gross pounced on the poor ape family, and he ate them all up, right down to their tails. Nu? Go figure it out. Our simian ancestors have many other interesting customs. If you want to find them out, go ask an ape.

Evaporated Feet

THE MAN BEGAN TO EVAPORATE as he walked through the field one fine day. He had a strange sensation that he would evaporate into nothingness, and become air. But luckily he only evaporated up to his knees. He was frightened, and ran through the fields on his stumps, looking for help.

A girl saw him running and yelled, "Hey, kneeman, what happened to your legs?"

"I don't know, girlie," he said, "I'm just evaporating. Do you know who can help me?"

"Of course, an old philosophical witch who lives down the road can give you some legs."

"Thanks, girlie, and God bless you."

He hobbled over to the witch's thatched roof hut. The kneeman told the witch his story.

"Well, lucky you didn't evaporate all the way," the witch said. "The reason you are evaporating is that your mind is not pinned on anything."

"But I used to care about everything," said the kneeman.

"Well if you care about everything, then you must wind up caring about nothing," the witch said.

"That's silly,"

"It is? Because of it you lost your feet. Perhaps you want them back."

"Oh, I want them back more than anything in the world."

"Once you lose feet, they never grow back. The only thing I can do is make false feet from a tree in my backyard. If you have faith in the tree, the false feet will suffice; if you don't believe in anything, you will evaporate into nothing."

"Gee, you're nice. What do I owe you for these feet?"

"Forget it," the witch said, "if we ever meet again, we will discuss the price."

The kneeman walked out, in the direction of the setting sun, on his false feet. The feet served him well, for a while. But although he had a strong crutch and good wood, he eventually evaporated into nothingness.

P.S. Who doesn't?

Delivery Room Tension

THE ROOM WAS STERILE. The table was prepared for the delivery. He scrubbed his hands with carbolated soap. He dried with an antiseptic towel. He went over to the delivery table, sweat pouring off his temples. This was no ordinary delivery. Complications set in. A mistake could be fatal. You know why fathers are so nervous when they are in the waiting room? It's because the procreative process is so delicate. The slightest error can result in a deformity for life. But one must do the job, if life is to go on. He went over to the table and made the delivery. He worked all night. And when the delivery was completed, he saw the fruit of his labor, and it was deformed. He said, "Sheet, what a lousy story." But it was his. His own verbal child was born from the seeds of his suffering, and he loved it because it was his. He made it word crutches and an amphibological wheelchair. The neighbors thought that he was crazy. They called him names.

"Hey you, personifier of the story, drop dead."

"Hey you, word-head, get a job, you parasite."

But he didn't care. He fed his stories catchy phrases, fried fish, alliteration-lettuce, filet of soul and verbal-bergers. He played his children music on the symbol and liar. It's hard work. But you have to pay a price, if you don't want to raise a clod. Some of his kids grew up and matured. They went into the world, met ????, married, and in general, did tolerably well for themselves.

The Literary Agent

I HAVE WRITTEN, TOLD MY SOUL, and in so doing purged myself of a demon. Of course, I must bring my stories to a literary agent in order to have my ordeal evaluated. My purge is only valuable if it is an acceptable sin-offering to gods and agents.

So I pack my stories in a shoe box and go off to the agent's lair. Over the agent's door is a sign: UNHOLY THE TELLER, UNHOLY THE TALE. I enter.

"Welcome sir. Let me see your shoe box filled with goodies."

"Here, here dear agent, is my life's work. Make me an offer," I say.

"Hmm, dear writer, I see these pages are covered with blood. Did you bleed for the story, did you bleed for me?"

"Oh Yes!" I say, "The least possible commitment is one's soul. I gave all to it."

"Hmm," says the agent, "I'll pay you a penny a book. I'll give you five cents for your life's work."

I'm dumbfounded. All my blood, my sweat, my tears, for this. Nights without sleep. I denied life itself – the beauty, the wenches. When my heart sought joy, I stayed up at night and wrote and wrote. Only to the word I was wed, a poor bedmate, a royal screwing. And now this jerk only gives me a nickel.

"You bad man," I yell, "A nickel for my blood; this is what you offer. How can you do this, you bastard?"

The agent throws me out. I go home and shove the stories through an electric grinder. I line the bottom of my cradle with the shreds. I hop into the cradle with a bottle of warm soda and my collection of elephant photographs. I dream selected passages from the book of Lamentations.

The Saint and the Beggar

THE WORLD'S GREATEST SAINT was visited by the world's greatest beggar. The beggar asked for the saint's room. The saint gave it. The beggar borrowed the saint's car and the saint's clothes. "I need a woman," said the beggar, "lend me your wife." The saint could not refuse. The beggar took more and more. The saint had less and less.

At the dinner table the beggar ate all the food. The beggar got fat, the saint got thin.

When the beggar took everything from the saint but his body he said, "Give me your body." The saint could not refuse. The beggar dived into the saint's body. They became one. The beggar consumed the inmost parts of the saint. When nothing was left of the saint, the beggar consumed all the possessions of the saint. He devoured the saint's wife, children, house and everything in sight.

When nothing was left, the beggar devoured himself.

So it is written: "If I am not for myself, who will be for me? And if I am only for myself, what am I?"

The Suspension

A STRING IS SUSPENDED IN AIR. It goes up deep into the sky. To the lower end of the string is tied a man. The man sways back and forth and hears the music of the symbol and liar. He is very nervous, for if his string breaks, he will fall from – I don't know what – I don't know where.

On other strings are attached various multicolored fruit, red cherries, blue grapes, yellow bananas and tan nuts. The fruit swing back and forth. Each fruit hangs by its own string.

On some strings hang bad boys; they have sticks in their hands. If they happen to swing by the man, they give him a good whack.

The situation is so unbearable that the man is almost ready to cut his own string. Why wait? The man does not cut himself off, for things keep passing by. As he swings on his string he takes notice of events: a lemon floats by, a cherry enters his mouth, he gets a good swat from the stick. If he breaks his string he may miss something. And of course, he doesn't believe that he can be restrung. So the fear of missing something keeps him suspended. In some ways you can see the man was lucky, for he was given a ticket to an infinite show (he did not even purchase the ticket). The heads of the suspended are in the shape of question marks. It is hilarious. But no one sees himself. There are no mirrors: just people, sticks, and fruit. Enjoy the stringed man. To hate him will be like hitting him with the stick. And that will be done anyway.

Waiting for the Mailman

EVERY DAY I CHECK THE MAILBOX to see if someone would send me a letter. The big part of the day was to look for the morning message. "Oh, Mr. Mailman, do I have a letter today? If I don't receive a letter, I surely will die." The mailman knows I need a letter from the outside. Stupid civil servant, what does he care about human suffering? I need mail or else I'll evaporate.

For the past ten weeks, I have not received a letter from anyone. I live in a cave and drink goat's milk. I've read all the books in the cave. I'm sick and tired of reading. All the books are cookbooks. The stove is broken. There is only goat's milk in the cave. What can I cook? There is nothing to do around here. Yesterday I rinsed my socks in goat's milk. Then I gave myself a hotfoot with a long match so I should be surprised. I reread the cookbook-the section on pie- CREAM PIE. I walked around the cave a few times and went to sleep. Oh, tomorrow I may get a letter from someone. I'll go to bed early so I'll be ready for the mailman. Some sweet luscious mail will set things right. The next day the mailman comes again.

"Mr. Mailman, what about today, huh?"

"I have nothing for you, you silly old fool."

"Not even an advertisement?"

"No, I have nothing for you."

And off he goes. I wish I had a dog that could bite his leg. Mrs. Kretch gets mail, Mr. Goopey gets mail. The whole world gets mail, but all I get is goat's milk. Alas, second-raters receiving first-class mail, and I don't even get a catalogue from Sears Robuck.

My mailbox is always empty. I don't even get a postcard. So I write myself a letter and send it away. A few days later I get up to see if there is any mail. And guess what? There is a letter for me. Oh, Joyous day!

But the postman will not be deceived. He suspects the letter is from me. He calls the police. The chief of police comes with his lackeys and two large German shepherd dogs.

"You are under arrest," he says. "You have addressed yourself. In our country that is a crime."

"But I only wanted a friend," I say.

"That's no excuse," the chief of police says. "This letter is all nonsense written in your own script. You'll swing for this." He leads me off to the van. Oh, this is terrible. I wanted to receive a message…a map. A map to another land. A land where the sun is shining, a place where the mailbox is overflowing. I wanted to go to the post office beyond the sea, the home of words. That place that everyone hopes to reach, and no one ever does.

The Private Eye

A STRANGER CAME TO MY OFFICE, he was looking for a detective.

"What can I do for you?" I asked.

"I lost something very important and I want to find it."

"What did you lose?"

"I don't exactly know."

"Where did you lose it?"

"I'm not sure."

"What did it look like?"

"I don't know."

"You must be joking. I can't find it unless you're more specific."

"I'm not sure I lost anything."

"Then why are you bothering me?"

"Because I have a sense of loss."

"Well, what will you give me, if I find it?"

"I don't know what the reward should be because I don't know what I lost."

"Why should I look for it, if I don't know what I'll get?"

"You should look because the reward may be great."

"That sounds logical to me. I'll take the job."

One day I brought the client a tree from India.

"Client, is this it?"

I brought thousands of things to the client: fingernails from Afghanistan, eggs from Romania, pots from Pakistan, screwdrivers from Siberia; nothing was right. I even tried to bring the client qualities that he might be missing:

A beautiful Ms., the incarnation of LOVE.

An orthodox theologian, the personification of TRUTH.

An academic professor, the embodiment of WISDOM.

Nothing I showed the client was right. Damn it! I don't know what it is, but I'm quite sure something definitely is missing. Out of curiosity, and like a fool, I go searching the world looking; I probably will never find it, and if I do, I have no idea what the reward will be.

Why Am I Not Marc Chagall?

MY PICTORIAL INTEREST WAS INITIATED by a jar of peanut butter cookies. About two years ago, I was a prominent lexicographer for a first-rate dictionary. One night, when I came home for supper, a horsefly buzzed my ear. I chased the creature away, but it came back and buzzed again… and again. I rolled the *New York Post* into a bat and chased the fly to the wall. It stopped on a high shelf, atop a jar of cookies. I slammed the jar with the *Post*. The cookie jar fell on my head and I was knocked out. I lay on the floor all night, next to a dead horsefly, in a pool of blood, amidst fragmented cookies. When I awoke, I felt there was a gong in my head being continuously banged by seventeen Ethiopian athletes.

I returned to work, but I couldn't concentrate on words. My boss suggested that I see a head doctor. That night I went to Ratner's on Second Avenue. I tried to forget my headache with sumptuous food: mushroom soup and black bread, potato latkes and sour cream, vegetable roast with kasha, coffee and cheesecake. After I ate, I still had a headache. I knew something was really wrong.

I asked Louie, the waiter, if he knew a head doctor. Waiters at Ratner's know everything.

"Pankey is the best doctor in New York," Louie said.

"Who's he?"

"He's an old guy who practices over a fortune-teller store on Delancey Street. He's a little crazy, but he only charges five bucks. He also does income tax as a sideline."

"How good could he be, if he makes out income tax?"

"Lissen. I once hurt my back. I was walking around like a camel. I went to twenty-five dollar specialists. They could do nothing. And Pankey cured me."

"What was wrong?"

"I was sleeping on a lumpy mattress."

"Big deal, anyone could have told you that."

"Lissen. The specialists didn't know it... and Pankey only charges five bucks. What do you have to lose?"

"OK I'll go tomorrow."

"Ya can't. He's only open on Wednesday and Friday."

"Only two days?"

"He ain't interested in money, only people."

"Then why does he do income tax?"

"For fun, and only in tax season."

"I'll make an appointment."

"He don't take appointments, first come, first serve."

"It doesn't sound kosher to me."

"OK then don't go. He don't need you. You need him." Louie went off to deliver a blintz.

I left Ratner's and went to bed. My head was ablaze. Firecrackers took off in my skull. Roman candles exploded. Bright red, smoking stars floated down over the waters of my soul. Rockets crashed into my cranium. And strangely enough, though everything sounded awful, it looked beautiful.

II.

Friday I went to Pankey. The office was a dump. He called me into the examination room. He was a sloppy little man wearing a sweatshirt and tennis shoes. He gave me a thorough examination: head, heart, lungs, nose, blood, knees, eyes, and toes.

"Why are you looking at my feet, if my head hurts?" I asked.

"Because everything is connected," he said.

"It is?"

"Sure. You can get a headache from bad posture, or tight underwear." Pankey gave me passages to read from a cookbook and asked me to remember the ingredients in certain stews and roasts. I couldn't remember much at all. He then had me select photos that would best express the feelings inspired by certain pastries. I did perfectly on that test.

"These tests I invented are foolproof," Pankey said. "Your headache will go away in a few days, but your problem won't."

"What's wrong?"

"You happen to have a rare disease caused by the fall of a blunt object on the cranium and the habit of living. It's called Weltzshmertz Syndrome. Each center of the brain controls a certain function. The verbal center of your brain has been damaged. Unfortunately you will find it increasingly difficult to deal with words."

"Oh, that's terrible. I work for a dictionary. My business is with words."

"Too bad. Occasionally, you will get a flash and your word power will be perfect. But eventually your ability to handle words will be zero. Fortunately you also had some luck. There is a medical phenomenon known as compensation. Deaf people sometimes develop exceptional touching ability. The blind sometimes have improved hearing. If someone has a leg shorter than the other, he also may have a leg longer than the other to even up the score. In your case, the visual senses are improving to compensate for the decline in the ability to handle words."

"Is there anything I can do?"

"Get a 35 mm camera. I suggest that you take pictures of old friends if you want to remember them. When your verbal and intellectual abilities almost disappear, you will still be excited by pictures. I also suggest that you take up painting or sculpture."

"I'm forty-six. I'm too old."

"You're not too old. Look at Grandma Moses. Anyhow pictures are better than words. It's easier to look than to talk. To make sentences strains the brain. I'm a man of few words myself. The examination is over. Five bucks."

Pankey stuck out his hand. I gave him five and left. I went to my office; I tried to write. I couldn't. I kept forgetting where to put the commas. My spelling was atrocious. I wanted to write a letter to Dr. Rosa Mishkin, a voluptuous Slavic woman, who was an expert on Russian entries. I just couldn't get the right words together. I called Rosa and invited her to lunch.

I met the vivacious Rosa at Yonnah Schimmel's Knish Shop. It was romantic. We exchanged pleasantries. I gave her half of a cheery-cheese for a bite of a potato knish. We got down to business. I wanted to know why certain Slavic terms were adopted by Germanic languages.

"Why do we say 'Hok mir nisht a chainik,' in Yiddish? Why is the Slavic word *chainik* meaning "teakettle" adopted by Yiddish, and the Slavic word for "coffeepot" not used?"

"Because it's there."

"What kind of answer is that?" I asked.

"It's probably there because it sounds good. *Chainik* came into Yiddish the same way the word *shmata* meaning "rag" did. Listen, Sh-maata, sh..maata, shmaaata. Doesn't it sound sensuous?"

She had a way of talking that made me tremble all over. The knishes and sensual talk aroused me, yet I felt my verbal capacities were diminishing. How could I tell her? I remembered what Pankey said about my visual perceptions. There was a flash of genius. I dipped my pencil into the mustard. I made a quick sketch on the napkin, with mustard, of that part of the body most used in making love. I held the work of art before her eyes and smiled.

"Your place or mine?" she said.

"Mine!" We rushed off in a cab, to my pad. And in a glorious night of delight, I proved to the fair Rosa Mishkin that I was not too old to cut the mustard.

Rosa moved into my apartment. I loved her dearly. She was a Christmas present in May. Beauty, brains and kindness wrapped up in a silver package and tied with a golden ribbon. Rosa was working as a professor of linguistics at Columbia University. She made a pretty penny. I told her of my illness. She understood. She insisted that I quit my job at the dictionary and go to art school. She said that she would foot the bills 'til I could make it on my own. I enrolled at the Art Students League. I painted most of the day. At night Rosa would come home and cook supper. Then I would paint and she would read. Late at night we'd listen to music and go to bed. I lost complete interest in books. Occasionally she would ask questions that I could not answer. I never spoke. After a month or so she showed signs of irritation; a burnt blintz, watery borscht, a "headache." I knew she was unhappy.

"Something's wrong, Rosa. What's up?"

"It's you. You never talk anymore."

"You know about my sickness," I said.

"I know, but I just can't talk to the wall. I think you don't care about me."

"That's not true. Half the pictures I paint are of you. I see you in my mind as a picture...a beautiful picture. But, you are not words."

"Painting is a one-way street. It's what you do. I want to do things WITH you. At night, in bed, you just look at old photos."

"Uh...I have nothing to say." I went into the corner and perused slides of Etruscan armor. Rosa read a linguistics book by Chomsky.

The next few weeks were unbearable. Rosa gave me an ultimatum: I must talk to her every night for fifteen minutes or she would leave. It was difficult. I couldn't come up with any words. Finally she left. Before she split, I took two dozen photos of her lovely body. I loved her dearly, yet every night I stood there gazing, frozen-tongued. I didn't want her to go, yet I didn't have the power to ask her to stay. With each sentence I felt I was pulling a wagon loaded with rocks up a steep mountain.

Now I was in deep trouble. With Rosa gone, I quickly used up my savings. Painting is expensive, a tube of oil costs a few bucks. I went on welfare. It wasn't enough. I ate potatoes every day with an occasional chicken-wing thrown in. I bought day old bread and half-rotten vegetables. I tried experimenting with different media, since I couldn't afford paint. I covered a large canvass with furnace ashes, strawberry jam and motor oil. I worked day and night for a month. I put every ash and bit of jam in the right place. I called the painting *Man's Need.* I brought my work to Professor Pincus at the Art Student's League. He looked at the painting and said, "Throw it in the garbage can."

"I worked on it for a month," I said, deeply hurt.

"Everyone here works hard. Hard work itself don't make art. If you paint junk like this, you'll always be a bum."

"Well, you can kiss my ass," I said and left. In my moment of anger and illness, I couldn't think of an original epithet. I wanted to give a brilliant verbal argument for the merits of my painting... but of course, I couldn't. I walked the streets friendless and alone.

I did not paint for the next few weeks. Pincus crushed my painting passion. At home, in the evening, I didn't feel like reading, and I wasn't painting. I was bored stiff. I paced back and forth.

For a hobby I bought a few pounds of rice and counted the grains over and over. When the Chinese New Year came I made a large dish of chow mein and devoured my hobby. I was fed up with grains. The world seemed empty. My only pleasure was music. When I walked, I hummed. But there is no future in being a professional hummer. What could I do? I went back to Pankey.

When I walked into Pankey's office, I was surprised to see him in an elegant blue suit, watering petunias. Last time I saw him he was wearing a torn sweatshirt, or was memory failing?

"Back again? I thought I cured you," he said, while sprinkling a bud.

"You look different," I said.

"Sure. Last time I was wearing rags. I change clothes to set a mood. If I put a crown on your head you would become a king. Nu, what's botherin' you?"

"My girl left me, I have cramps and a headache, I'm broke, and worst of all, Pincus the painter rejected my paintings."

"Well, what's your problem?"

"Waddya mean. I'm climbing the walls! I wanted to be another Marc Chagall. Why can't I be a Chagall?"

"That's easy. You can't be him, because he's a him and you is a you."

"Just the point. I don't know what to be. I once knew words, but that went out. Then I was a painter, but it seems that's no good."

"So invent something else."

"But I'm getting older."

"Who doesn't?"

"And I'm unhappy."

"Who isn't?"

"And I don't know enough."

"Who does?"

"Once you told me my visual senses would improve, but I feel the colors are fading. Red is less red. Blue is less blue."

"With time, everything fades."

"I want intensity."

"So sit on a tack."

"I'm suffering. Help me! I don't need jokes."

"I don't joke. I just can't take a kvetch. What do you like?"

"Uh, music, I guess."

"OK, I'll test you in music." Pankey looked in my ears and tapped my head. Then he put some electrodes on my skull and played records of symphonic and rock music. After the test he wrote a prescription.

"Follow the prescription and you'll be OK for a while."

"Why only a while?"

"Because no medicine lasts forever. Life is fatal."

I looked at the prescription, it said: PLAY THE DRUM IN A ROCK BAND.

"Are you crazy? I'm too old."

"Nonsense. Casals is over ninety, and he got a young wife to boot."

"I don't know how to play the drum."

"You like music, so learn."

"But why the drum?"

"Why not? If I said play the piano, you'd say, 'Why shouldn't I play the guitar?' I picked the drum to make it easy. You're getting older. You don't have too much time to fiddle around."

"Where will I get a drum?"

"My nephew was just drafted. He played in a rock band. I can give you the whole set for twenty bucks and I'll throw in the price of a visit."

"Can I make a living from playing the drum?"

"If you're good enough. My cousin Hymie has a pizza place in the Bronx. He needs a waiter. You can work as a waiter to get by. If you make it as a drummer, fine. If not, you'll still be a waiter."

In desperation I took Pankey's advice. I became a decent waiter, and I got a job with an orthodox rock group known as THE SONS OF PURIM. Three nights a week, I pound out my soul on a red snare drum. I wear a long black wig and a silver skullcap. Menachem Mendel, leader of the band, yells when I'm off beat. I can take it. After all, THE SONS OF PURIM ain't the Philharmonic, and Mendel is not Segovia.

Five days a week, I serve pizza and spaghetti. Admittedly, I'm no big shot, but who really is? I've slowly grown to like what I'm doing. The things about us fall away, and so do we. But in a short time, I've loved music, the words of the dictionary, passionate women and the blue sky.

Pankey was right, the holiday of the senses must end. My trunk is packed and my clothes are pressed. I don't look for the boat. When it comes, it comes. Meanwhile, music must be made in this lovely agony and dream: my life.

How To Score with a Chick

BILL CARTWRIGHT, THE REAL ESTATE DEVELOPER, was fairly content with his life. He had a beautiful wife and lived in the nicest home in town. His twin children, Tim and Tip, were first and second in the junior class at Harding High. Tim was captain of the football team, and Tip was president of the debating society.

Bill had inherited four million dollars from Ebeneezer Cartwright Jr., his frugal stepfather, who had made a fish fortune from crabs. Bill invested his patrimonious profit properly and prospered. All was well with Bill until he became suspicious of Mary, his loving wife.

Mary Cartwright was into doing good. She led cookie bakes for homeless Hungarians and booked benefits for broken Bohemians. Also she worked as a volunteer at the community hospital. Usually Mary would come home from the hospital at six and make supper. Lately she was coming home at nine or ten with the claim that she "had to work late." She seemed to be aloof. At night in bed, she did not participate in sex with the same gusto and relish and mustard. She would say "later" or "I'm not in the mood," or "I have a toothache."

Mr. Cartwright was taken aback by her affront, so he took her aside and said, "Something is up." She did not get the gist of his argument. Cartwright became suspicious. He loved her dearly. He would do anything for her. Perhaps it was...Oh, No! He did not want to think of that. But the coming home late and no sex. COULD IT BE ANOTHER MAN?

He could not quell questioning her queasiness and he felt he was quite quaszy.

Mr. Cartwright hired a detective to put a tail on Mary. He felt that he had to find out if she was a cheater. He could not bear being a cuckold. He was planning to kill her or her lover, if something fishy was up.

The detective, a Mr. Green, called a few days later with the report. "I watched your wife leave work every day at six with Dr. Faraday."

"What did they do next?"

"They went to a sleazy hotel at the East End."

"And then what happened?"

"They went upstairs, I saw a light go on in a room and then the light went out immediately. The light was out for one hour. Then they both came downstairs. Your wife was adjusting her skirt and Dr. Faraday kissed her."

"Does it look suspicious?" Cartwright asked.

"Yeah, it don't look kosher to me."

"Oh I'd like to punch that guy Faraday right in the kisser."

"I hate to tell you this, Cartwright, but Faraday is a lady doctor."

"Do you mean…"

"Well if it 'ill make you feel any better, Faraday is a masculine woman."

"Thanks for the information. You'll get a check tomorrow," Cartwright said, as he hung up the phone dejectedly. He was a broken man. His own Mary running around and cheating with a woman. He didn't know what to do. He decided to follow on one of her trysts on Tuesday, and untangle the web of womanish deceit. He would try to woo her from her woman lover, for he felt he could not live without her.

One Tuesday he wore a trench coat and a wide-brimmed fedora. He stood across the street from the hospital at six. Mary exited with a masculine looking woman who was carrying a doctor's bag. Ah, Dr. Faraday, it was true. He stealthily followed Mary and Faraday to a sleazy hotel. They walked up the stairs hand in hand. He waited fifteen minutes and charged up the stairs. He kicked in the door with one tremendous boot. There they were, both of them, naked, doing things that he could not believe.

"So Mary, what do you have to say about this!" he yelled, pointed to the embarrassed Dr. Faraday whose Cuban panatela fell out of her mouth.

"I have nothing to say, Bill, I want a divorce," she said calmly, fingering her long flowing locks.

"Divorce?" He could not believe his ear. His left ear was deaf from a hunting accident.

"Yes, I love Jane Faraday," Mary said.

"You must be mad. She's a woman."

"Well, if you can like women, so can I," Mary said, sticking out her tongue.

"You'll never get a divorce," he said.

"We'll see about that. I'm going to my lawyer tomorrow. Now please leave. We are busy," she said.

He left in a huff and went home to do some soul-searching. He couldn't find any. He felt he was going crazy. He still loved her even though she threw him out for a woman. You can never trust a charity worker.

Mary got a divorce and moved into a garden apartment with Dr. Faraday. Cartwright was despondent. He felt he must have Mary at any price. At first, he thought that if she were away a while he would get used to being without her. But the longer she stayed away, the more he seemed to miss her.

One day, while reading *Time*, he came across an article about research being done at Johns Hopkins University on men who were being changed into women. An operation can be performed where the male sexual organ is removed and female hormones are injected. The men grow breasts, the voice goes up, the hair on the chest comes off, and presto, the man becomes a woman, or a reasonable facsimile. Although Cartwright felt comfortable as a man all his life, a strange thought occurred to him that he tried to suppress. The thought kept coming back again and again: IF SHE WON'T HAVE ME AS A MAN, WOULD SHE HAVE ME AS A WOMAN... IF SHE WON'T HAVE ME AS A MAN, WOULD SHE HAVE ME AS A WOMAN? The more he thought of it, the more logical it seemed.

Even if he failed, instead of being a rich unhappy man he would be a rich unhappy woman, and if he succeeded it would certainly be worthwhile. He decided to go ahead with the sex transformation.

Cartwright went to Dr. Heinrich Pankey, the well-known Crypto-German psychiatrist. At first Dr. Pankey was opposed to the operation.

"Ze operation can only be performed on zoes who are psychologically udder biologically a voman. You is chust an unhappy man," Dr. Pankey said.

"I must have this operation. I'm willing to give you fifteen grand if you say that I am in critical need of this operation."

"Vell, in dat case anyvun villing to pay fifteen gran iz psycholudgically a voman. Und anudder problem is dat you'll have to spend a munt in Baltimore, und dat shudn't happen to a dog."

"Pankey, I'll even spend a month in Baltimore. I'm willing to do anything."

"Gut. I'll write up a teknikel paper saying dat der shmuk must be removed for psychic reasons. I use a lodda big voids, dat aways does it. All dough I tawk like dis, I write like dis." Pankey then showed Cartwright a technical article that was almost unreadable.

"Do you mean to say psychiatrists can read this article?" Cartwright asked.

"Of cus not. Dey don't wanna look dum, so day don't qvestion me. Since I have a repatation, I can get avay mit moider. Und pleez pay in kesh, I don't wanna pay too much ze incum tex."

Bill Cartwright went to Baltimore and had his operation. He did not turn into a beautiful woman, in fact he was a rather ugly woman, but a woman. She bought a green mini-skirt, a pink blouse, an alligator handbag and a new pair of high-heel boots. Bill never had much taste in any gender. She hurried back to the town of Harding to re-court the fair Mary. Bill went to the same house where Mary had her tempestuous tryst with the mesomorphic Dr. Faraday. Bill kicked in the door. And guess what? Mary was in bed. Was she in bed with Dr. Faraday? No. SHE WAS IN BED WITH A GOD DAMN CHICKEN! Bill Cartwright could not believe her eyes or nose.

"Who are you?" shrieked the frightened Mary, and the chicken clucked some nonsense.

"It's me, your former husband, I've become a woman for you," Bill said in her soprano voice.

"You shouldn't have gone to the trouble," Mary said.

"Why not?"

"I don't care for you as a man or a woman," Mary said. The chicken nodded with approval.

"Who is this chicken I see you with?" Bill asked.

"It is Barton Feinstein, my new lover." The chicken smiled.

"Chickens, Yuuck! How could you do such a thing?"

"You, what do you know of true love? Humans, they're all alike. All they want is things," Mary said.

"But look at all the trouble I went through. It cost me fifteen grand."

"It's your hard luck. Barton and I have things to discuss. Please leave." Mary kicked Bill into the street. Bill was a lost soul. Foiled by a chicken. Cast out into the cruel world by a twenty-nine cent per pound fryer. Ah, the injustice of it all.

Bill rented a dingy room in a dump in Dubuque for a dollar a day. Alone and friendless in the cruel world, Bill took to reading books on mysticism. Bill felt useless as a man and as a woman. Bill was still madly in love with Mary. If there was only a way to turn Barton Feinstein into chicken fricassee. Fortunately Bill came across an article in a local paper by one Rajput Singh, Sikh mystic from Punjab. The advertisement was as follows:

"Reincarnation specialist: Rajput Singh. Return to earth as animal of your choice. Why gamble with eternity? Learn mystery of the East. Come back as lion, tiger, duck or chicken. Satisfaction assured. Group rates. Free magic robe with all lessons. This is legitimate. No weirdoes or kooks need apply. Box 472 Dubuque."

Bill thought, she won't have me as a man, she won't have me as a woman; she WILL have me as a CHICKEN! She thought of the Sikh and remembered the old saying, *Sikh and ye shall find.* Bill wrote to Rajput Singh and got the whole reincarnation kit for fifty bucks. According to Rajput, to be reincarnated as a chicken, one must think only of chickens, one must concentrate on chickens. Then when one dies, one will come back as a chicken, or at the very least a duck.

One day, at the hen house, when Bill was watching a Rhode Island Red, she slipped on some chicken-dung and fractured her skull. Bill was dead. Now the test. Was Singh a fraud? Bill felt her brain leave her body and enter a giant egg. Ah, it was true. One CAN believe what one reads in the papers. Bill broke through the shell and came out a fine chick. It took a little while for the feathers to straighten out. Bill was now too young for Mary. She hung around the chicken house 'til the age of mating, and then went quickly to Mary's pad. Bill flew in the window of Mary's living room. Mary was there discussing business with Barton Feinstein.

"It's me, Bill, I'm a chicken, for you Mary…I did it all for you."

"You shouldn't have gone through the trouble," Mary said.

"Why not?" asked Bill.

"Because you're not my type of man, you're not my type of woman, and you're not my type of chicken," Mary said.

Barton clucked.

"Well, I've gone as far as I can. You know what Mary Cartwright? I didn't like you that much either. I was just blinded by passion. You can take Barton and shove him up your ass. Goodbye forever." Bill, for revenge, dropped a double-yolker that splattered on the rug, and flew out the window. Mary went about her business as if nothing happened. Now Bill was free as a bird. She flew down to Toms River, New Jersey and met a rooster named Wendel Kravitz. The new love melted the icy past into lukewarm water, under the bridge of life. Wendel and Bill flew off wing in wing, feather to feather, and did with relish what chickens do.

Confessions of the Great Orange Eater

AND SO IT WAS IN MY FIFTY-FIFTH YEAR as a teacher in a girl's high school that I decided to become young again. Not only young for the fair Anthea Fishbein, not young so I should deceive inevitable death, but young so I could believe in my own strength. If this world were an iron bar, I'd break it over my knee.

I have always kept a youthful appearance. My diet is one that very few people have the self control to maintain. Oranges and water for breakfast, wheat-germ and fresh fruit for lunch, skim-milk and goat curd for dinner. And at night two pitchers of dark beer. I took twenty vitamins every morning and did fifty-five push-ups and a few laps around the bed. I guess at fifty-five I could fool anyone into thinking I was fifteen years younger, but I felt that my time on this earth was running out.

I was doing research, in the girl's boarding school, on the stems of lilies. Although I had a PhD and a great deal of experience, I chose to teach at a boarding school for girls. I had a desire for young female companionship even though my thirty-five year old wife proved to be an ample partner.

Dr. Pankey, the mad biologist who hired me, was experimenting on the brains of animals. He had kept a spaniel alive for one year, with the brain of a terrier. The spaniel thrived and gave birth to twins. I had always toyed with the idea of transplanting a human brain. MY BRAIN! How I yearned for a new body. I knew my old tired body would not last with the young Anthea Fishbein. How I longed to have the wench. Oh, how I longed to be young and strong again. She was one to watch…to watch in her exuberant, youthful beauty, the beauty that I knew was fading from my life. Oh, my fast fading life. My body was decaying, but gazing on her made me young again.

I remember when she came to me with her problems.

"Oh, sweet Anthea, your special studies project in Biology 349 is a failure. Your hamsters won't eat lettuce." Oh the poor dear, with blonde flowing hair and pineapple breasts, had hamsters who could not eat lettuce.

Screw those hamsters, fair Anthea! It is I who should be feeding on thy love. I was not one to offend the sixteen-and-three-quarter year old bewitching tyke. I could not tell the young one of my great love. I told her to come to my office one night to discuss hamsters.

"Bring your hamsters Anthea, fear not the grades. Grades are made in heaven, and you will be had on earth. Oh, head divine."

That night Anthea came with her hamster cage. We talked shop. I invited her out for a strawberry ice cream soda. We joked and chatted. Ah, I was young again. And when I looked into her eyes I knew she was madly in love with me.

I wanted her to be near me all the time. For the sake of true love, I fired the young mice-feeder, Debbie Meltzer, and gave the job to Anthea. Anthea tended the mice nightly, from six to eight. I came and helped. She knew! She knew! The joy in my heart. One night, while she was feeding the mice, she looked more beautiful than ever. I couldn't resist. I grabbed her and kissed her passionately. My heart was on fire. She dug her nails into my back. And she said with all her heart, "I love you Mr. Plunkett," while the yellow moon shone through the window, and the gray mice squeaked to the joy of my joy.

Ah, sweet ecstasy of life. How unbounded was my joy. The romps in the sheets, the exuberance of her youth, the beauty of her face. The bliss of divine conjugation almost made me forget that my hair was graying and arthritis had begun stiffening the joints of my elbows. My mind always said "Yes," but my body was beginning to say "NO." So I lived in sweet misery until the fateful night of the spring prom. I was a chaperone. I the great orange-eater, a chaperone. I, the lover of life, a mere watcher.

The young Anthea danced with a Princeton freshman. I saw her looking into his eyes, I saw her admiring his young strong body. Oh, how I hated him. What did he know of love? What did he know of human passion and deep suffering? A mere pup, wet behind the ears.

Smiling at the fair Anthea who should be mine, and mine alone. Her looks should have been only for me, the long suffering and brilliant.

Ah, the fair haired Anthea, who walked beneath the moonlight, who brought joy to my old body, was now being led astray by a young fool. Then, again, I thought of my plan. Could I have his youthful body with my time-worn brain, I would have the wisdom of the old with the strength of the young. Then I would pull earth and sky together and ride off with the fair Anthea. I thought of Dr. Pankey. YES! MY BRAIN AND THE BODY OF RAMON FABER, PRINCETON TWERP! I knew I could not resist, even death itself would not stop me from having the fair wench, and I would be young again!

> Bid me weep, and I will weep,
> While I have eyes to see;
> And having none, Yet I will keep
> A brain to weep for thee.

I knew Ramon would go steady with my Anthea. I was right, every week he drove down in his fancy car, and took her for drinks beneath the willow trees. "No, No, Ramon Faber, you won't have the fair Anthea, not over my dead body, you won't." Then the final blow came. Anthea just blurted it out after mice feeding, one night. "Mr. Plunkett (she always kept a formal distance when it came to titles, even though we made love regularly), even though I love you very much, there is another man. I truly love Ramon Faber. You are a bit too old. When I am thirty-one, you will be seventy. I don't think there is any future in our relationship." "You're right," I said, "let's just be friends." She was shocked. I gave in too easily. Little did she know of my plan.

That night I went to see Pankey. I told him I wanted a new body. I wanted my brain transplanted into the body of Ramon Faber. I wanted to be young again. And have the fair Anthea forever. I WANTED HER TO BE MINE! ALL MINE! MINE AND MINE ALONE!

Dr. Pankey was mad. But competent. Pankey always wanted to transplant a human brain. It was his life's ambition. He had a PhD. In physical education. He was not allowed to cut up people. They let him teach freshman biology and coach the girls' field hockey team. The animal experiments done by Pankey were done in secret. Since he had been obsessed with animal brains, he had killed seventeen chickens, thirty-four cats, and forty dogs. Half of his transplants were successful. He warned me of the risks. But what did I have to lose? I was already fifty-five, and I had a chance of becoming eighteen. I did not want to go on without Anthea. With my super intellect, I could be the brightest student at Princeton. Life could be lovelier the second time around. As I talked to Dr. Pankey, his mad, wild eyes lit up. A fiendish grin was on his lips, a grin in the shape of an "S" sideways. He rubbed his hands together, tenderly. "Yes," he shrieked, "together we shall conquer death…field hockey, pfft. Shit!!"

The first part of my plan was to get to know Ramon Faber well. I wanted to know about his family, hobbies, friends and relatives. I would need all the data I could get before the transplant. I invited Anthea and Ramon over for dinner. Fortunately, Ramon was a poor student in English, a field wherein I excelled. I told him that I would help him with his themes. I had him write only biographical themes. I Xeroxed these papers and ran a colorful account of his life. Ramon was on the football team. I constantly probed about the details of the game. Finally I achieved enough information for the great day. One night, in May, Pankey and I drove down to Princeton. We went to Ramon's dorm. We told him we were passing by. We sat and talked. We invited Ramon to come for an anchovy pizza. The unwitting Ramon got into our truck. Ha sat between me and Pankey. Pankey slugged him over the head with a blackjack. And we were off to the secret laboratory at the girl's school.

There were two operating tables in the laboratory. Pankey had hundreds of surgical instruments, a machine for blood transfusions, a bank with fifty quarts of fresh blood, a heart-lung machine, tanks of oxygen, six boxes of fig bars to munch on during the operation and a collection of obscene photographs.

He told me the operation would take sixteen hours. I did not care. I did not care, as long as I had the chance of being born again. As long as the fair Anthea would be mine. The ether mask was placed on my face. I fell into a deep sleep and dreamt of eternal youth. After a while my mind went blank. I don't know how long I lay on the operating table. Eternities, moments, days, years. Time ceases to exist when the brain ceases to function. Slowly, slowly, my eyes opened. God, I thought, I'm still alive! I wiggled my fingers, I wiggled my toes, they worked! I raised my hand. It was a strong muscular hand. It was the hand of Ramon Faber! I tried to get up, but I had an awful headache. Pankey looked at me.

"Plunkett, a success! We made it. You must rest a little while longer."

"How long have I been here?"

"Two weeks. I've taken care of everything. I sent forged letters to Anthea with Faber's name, saying that he was depressed and that he would return in a few weeks. I also covered for you with Miss Fidgebit, our esteemed headmistress. I told her you had to go away to Florida because of an unexpected illness. It's OK, you'll be up and around in a few days." Pankey was right. In a few days I regained my strength. No, it was not my strength, it was his. I was strong. I was stronger than I ever was in my life, To celebrate, I bent a horseshoe. I had the voice, the body, the energy and the sexual power of Ramon Faber, and best of all, I had the mind of Edmund Plunkett. If I could have a transplant every twenty years or so, I could be practically immortal. The only true way to endure is to have continuity of the thinking brain. No man really lives on in his works or in his children. The only existence is continuous thought, thought that can consider, grow, remember and forget. With a young heart, pumping fresh blood to an old wise brain, reinvigorating the decaying calls, I had expectation of becoming the greatest genius of all time. And with a brain that had learned every sexual technique known to man and beast and a body of a young athlete, I had the possibility of being the best lay on the planet earth. My explosive thoughts speeded my recovery. I called the fair Anthea and told her of my car accident. With bandaged head I sped to the wench for whom I bled. I went to her room, and there she lay in bed with her teddy-bear, youthful, delectable and mine! I caressed her and made passionate love to her. LOVE AS NO MAN HAS MADE, BEFORE OR SINCE THE EXISTENCE OF THIS EARTH! Anthea could not believe it.

"Ah, Ramon how could you be so good?"

"Practice, just practice." We spent two weeks in bed, and then I went to Princeton to "return" to my studies. It was a perfect switch. No one ever expected a Plunkett brain in a Faber body. The teachers could not understand the improvement in my grades. I went from a B- to an A+ in a short time. Knowing all the tricks of manners and human behavior, I became the most popular student on campus. However, as things got better, things started to get worse. I was the president of a fraternity. The games we played seemed childish. The talk in the corridor of the school was dull. I didn't care whether or not we won a football game. Although I played well, what did it matter?

And even, even the fair Anthea began to wither. The flower without whom I thought I could not exist, began to decay, petal by petal. To live forever is to constantly do over that which already has been done. I would again go to college, I would again marry, I would do everything again. God! What for? Only when it was not available did immortality appear to be the greatest prize. But alas, the old brain knows too much. It could not wipe out the sad wisdom that comes with old age. For, if one's body does not decay, the world still does. The ugliness and the suffering go on and on. What a bore, to see constant re-runs of the same show. It would be a pleasure to observe moral improvement, but it looks like only machines get better. For me, one life is enough.

So, as I once bid myself to stay, now I ask myself to go. I am in a cheap hotel in Philadelphia. I have just drunk orange juice and sleeping pills. In one hour I will go down to the beach, and float out to sea on a rubber raft. There I will die. My advice to those who are considering resurrection is, don't bother. As I float out on the raft, for my last journey, smile on my face and rubber duck in hand, I will dream again of the fair Anthea, with blue eyes and golden hair.

Diana of the Duds

"Oh, let there be nothing on earth but laundry,
Nothing but rosy hands in the rising steam
And clear dances done in the sight of heaven."
Richard Wilbur

RESNICK LIVED FOR HIS LAUNDRY. Since he quit his job as a postal clerk his existence centered around cleaning clothes.

It wasn't a bad life. On Monday, WASH DAY, he would assemble his weekly underwear and shirts; he wore a set of underwear daily. The sheets were changed every two weeks.

Resnick went to a laundry about an hour's drive from the city. It was a modern automatic laundry. The kind where you put twenty-five cents in the machine and music is piped in. In fact, this laundry had a soda machine and a color television. A stack of books was on the table near the dryer. The place was usually busy on Monday. That was GOOD.

Resnick carried his bundle into the store. All the machines were taken. That was very GOOD. Resnick bought a Coke and Hershey Bar and thumbed through the *Reader's Digest.* Finally a washer was empty. Resnick dumped his clothes in the washer and watched the colors spin round. It was a pretty sight. Resnick thumbed through *Good Housekeeping* when the laundry was done. He discussed bleaches with an old woman. Very interesting.

Resnick stopped off at a coffee shop on the way home and bought *The Evening Post.* He walked around for an hour and looked at store windows. When he got home he cooked a can of cheap spaghetti, and read and reread the newspaper. It was Monday evening. THE FIRST DAY. Resnick watched *The Late Show* until he went to sleep. His laundry was still wet. Resnick never used the dryer on Monday, for Tuesday would be drying day.

Tuesday morning Resnick arose bright and early. There would be good laundry to do. He went for breakfast to a distant diner. On the way home after breakfast, he stopped at an air-conditioned supermarket. It was beautiful. He walked up and down the rows of neatly stacked cans. Every ham hock in the meat counter was in order. The bread section smelled good. The best section was the coffee. Resnick went to the coffee grinder and sniffed. Excellent. But Resnick was a busy man. It was 10 am. He hurried home and put the damp wash out on the line. He sat down with The Times and watched his shirts dry. He took a lunch break, tuna fish and lima beans, and went back to laundry watching.

Resnick dreaded Wednesday. IRONING DAY. But in every life a little rain must fall. Tuesday's laundry was done. Another day lived through. GOOD. Tuesday night Resnick cooked a can of ravioli and he read the papers. Tuesday was a good TV night but Resnick went to bed early.

On Wednesday Resnick got up at 7 am. He looked at the sign over his bed—CLEANLINESS IS NEXT TO GODLINESS—and washed himself thoroughly. He stretched his breakfast by baking potatoes. He washed the floor and ironed the clothes slowly. Most of Wednesday was over. GOOD. He ate the evening meal and watched some good TV.

Thursday was brilliant. DRY CLEANING DAY. Only a dollar seventy-five for a week's dry cleaning. The cleaners had the latest magazines and the place was air-conditioned. Resnick never had the dry cleaning pressed on Thursday; he always saved that for Friday. After Friday's pressing he was pooped. Resnick did not take Saturday off. He mopped the floors, washed the car and rinsed a few things. Sunday was the day of rest. He just hung around the house thinking of his duds. He subscribed to the *Hand Laundryman* and the *Dry Cleaner's Annual*. He leafed through a steam laundry journal and looked at pictures of extractors.

And so he let his flim-flam days glide by in the ecstasy of cleanliness. He realized that when his unemployment insurance ran out he would have to get a job. He planned on driving a cab three or four nights a week. That would be enough to keep the machine going, pay for the soap, clothes and food. Resnick was no spendthrift. He was thirty and in good health and all he wanted from life was to be fed and keep clean.

Then one fateful day it happened. He was doing his duds, when in she walked in all her laundering loveliness. She was pretty but not beautiful, clean looking and wholesome. She wore a tight blouse, freshly cleaned, and neatly pressed dungarees. She took the machine three numbers down from Resnick. The laundry that she loaded in the machine was the clothes for one person. THAT WAS GOOD. He did not see a ring on her finger. That was VERY GOOD. She washed her duds, put them in the dryer, folded them neatly, in his presence, and left. There was a look in her eye that attracted his attention. It was a clean sad look. For some reason, he spent a good part of the following week thinking of her. He hoped that she would return and that he could talk to her about some bleach or discuss fabric-softeners. Perhaps she would have a rinse problem. He was shy. He could discuss laundry with anyone on the most sophisticated levels, but other topics frightened him. He was a man of few words and he had no friends. The following Monday he washed himself thoroughly and he took an extra close shave. He had some dirty socks that he took out of his laundry bundle, thinking that she would not appreciate the stains. He rinsed the dirty socks at home and dried them in the oven. He quickly drove to the laundry, put his clothes in the washer, and thumbed through a copy of *Life*. In she walked, and took a machine right next to his. He liked that very much. She sat down at his side and looked at a newspaper. He wanted to talk to her but he did not know what to say. He was afraid that she would be shocked if he just started a conversation. Perhaps she never spoke to strangers. If she would only do something wrong; if her machine would overflow, he could come to the rescue. Nothing happened. He did not want to lose the opportunity to speak; perhaps she would never come back. He had to say something.

"Pardon me Miss," he said, "do you have change of a dollar?"

"No," she said, and smiled. He did not know what else to say. Actually, had she given him change, he would have felt forced to dry his clothes in the machine, something he did not want to do.

He took his clothes and left. He was happy that she smiled. THAT WAS VERY GOOD. He thought maybe she liked him. He thought of her more deeply that week. He felt that he was falling in love. At first he thought it was silly. After all, he only observed her twice in the laundry, through two wash loads and one dry. But Isn't love a mad passion? He felt that there was no need for further explanation. If only he could do something to win her over. He thought of asking her to a movie, but he was afraid. If only he could do something to impress her. He gulped down his can of tuna fish and considered writing a poem in her honor. That is the way to win women, he thought. He did not even know her name. He chose the name Diana because he thought it was pretty, and he wrote what he considered to be a sweet, sad ballad. Women always like sad songs. He called his song:

Diana of the Duds

While doing my duds
I spied fair Diana
Stacking her towels
Alone in a laundry.
I'll buy her a Pepsi
And sing of white linen
'til two in the morning
when no one is near.
Come clean my Diana,
We'll run to the suburbs
And sing about bluebirds
Far from the dust of my home.
I'll get you a powder
Of enzyme and power
And our glasses will sparkle
Like the sun on your hair.
Alas, there's a mound
Of uncleanable linen
That keeps fair Diana
Away from my suds.

Come clean my Diana,
I'll sing you of rosebuds.
There is a deep dirt
No bleach will take out.
There is a deep hurt
No bleach will take out.

Resnick was pleased with his creation. Perhaps, if he could get to know her, he would present her with the poem. He prayed that she would return to the laundry and that he would get up the courage to make a move.

The week flew by. Monday he was in the laundry earlier than usual. The poem was folded in his back pocket. He brought an extra package of non-pollutant soap which he would use as a come-on. Diana always used improper detergent flakes. Diana arrived looking more lovely than ever. She placed the clothes in the washer and inserted her inferior flakes. Resnick took a deep breathe, walked up and said, "Pardon me Miss, you should use non-pollutant soap. Ah…I happen to have an extra package of this." He thrust the package into her hand. His heart beat quickened. Would she accept his suds?

"Well, I don't know," she said, "you had to pay for the soap. I don't want it for nothing."

"Take it. Consider it a present."

"Thanks a lot. How much do I put in."

"The whole package."

"Thanks again."

She placed his suds in her duds. They both sat looking at the machine. This will not do, he thought. He had to say something. "I haven't seen you around this laundry. I'm a regular. Do you live around…here?" he asked.

"No, I like downtown. I'm staying in my boyfriend's house. He's away in the reserves."

"Oh," said Resnick, and he buried his head in *Time Magazine.* CURSES! She deceived him by doing laundry for one. Another outsider had disturbed his balance. He did not wait for the second rinse. He withdrew his threads in a huff and left. She was not that pretty anyhow. Now he had wasted a night writing a poem. And it had cost him a package of suds. He decided not to get involved again.

He arrived home earlier than usual. He did not know what to do. He baked a cherry pie and scrubbed the oven thoroughly. He read the papers and looked at the calendar. DRAPE TIME was approaching, also the floors had to be rewashed and the bedspreads hadn't been done in two weeks. The rug would be a major venture. There were still interesting things left in the world.

He say down wearily with a cup of cocoa and a book on tennis which he never played. He thought of tomorrow. It would be DRYING DAY! A smile came to his lips. It would be FINE.

Love Tale

I CAME TO HARVARD THE HARD WAY. I had neither big money nor fantastic grades. I graduated from Midwood High School with an 87 average. Not bad, but not great. I knew Harvard could bring status and money, and most of all high-class ass. I leafed through the Harvard catalogue like it was the Holy Bible. The thought of shtupping someone at Radcliffe made me tingle all over. That's right, me, Harvey Gross, son of Mendel the bagel baker, porking a Radcliffe. Not revenge, but envy was my motive. It is written: "He who fucks two rungs up the ladder rises two rungs himself."

To knock-up a "Cliffie" would be no tragedy. What's wrong with getting a few dollars without breaking your back. My father got bad feet from standing over a hot bagel oven all day. He got varicose veins. That should happen to all the Nazis.

Well, as I said before, I didn't get into Harvard on my grades alone. First, I was in the army. In Korea I pulled a few deals. I sold a truck and part of a field hospital. I also did a bit of money lending. 100 percent pay day stakes. That means, for a ten dollar loan you get twenty back on pay day. I got out of the army with five grand and the GI Bill. I could have come home with three times as much if I didn't have to pay off a C.I.D. investigator. Anyway, a veteran on the GI Bill got a better chance of getting into Harvard than an ordinary shmuck.

Now I pulled my ace bit. There was a crazy guy in the neighborhood by the name of Glickman. Sometimes he would talk to his shoe; he would scream from the windows; he would make a phone call by dialing his coffee cup. In the summer he would wear a heavy coat; in the winter he'd walk outside in a thin sweater. Like many crazy people he knew thousands of odd facts. He was a brilliant student at City College before he flipped. I knew that if he could hold on for a few hours, he could still rack up on the college boards. It was risky. But he came through like a champ and I was on my way.

It is written: "He who cheats without getting caught, is more honest than he who doesn't cheat and gets caught."

I had no qualms whatever about cheating. One of Harvard's most famous graduates got kicked out for cheating, and then went on to become a U.S. Senator. Nathaniel West went through Brown on someone else's records. I'm smarter than most people, why shouldn't I have a little bit of the gravy? I know life is difficult. Each bagel Mendel baked had a tear from his only eye. I was not my father's son. I saw great things.

My plan was simple. I wanted to get as much out of this short life as possible; I wanted to ride with the Brahmins; I wanted to walk on the waters; and with all that, I still did not want to extinguish the flame. To be honest, I'm a noble man. I believe that each man is unique and that each one has hidden in himself something beautiful and true that is his alone. We are the children of a king and our duty is to find the hidden message. And one of the messages I heard was: "Rip off some rich son-of-a-bitch and set your poppa up in a condominium at Miami Beach." Let me tell you one thing, there is a lot of money to go around, and too many fuckers got more than their share. A lot of these fuckers got their dough through inheritance or theft, and I was going to even out the score a bit.

I moved into a dorm at Harvard and that was a mistake. The freshmen were mostly like babies. They didn't know on which sides their asses were buttered. They'd play their shitty music at night and give me a headache. I wanted to do business, I didn't want to be with noisy kids. I put an ad in Boston After Dark:

"KERD LITERARY SERVICES

Theses, term papers, written and typed by M.A. Ivy League.

Magna Cum, 'B' guaranteed.

$3.00 per page.

130 ½ Beacon Street"

Of course the part about the M.A. was bullshit. I was a freshman. But who ever checks? I got twenty orders the first week. I hired a guy for two dollars a page to do some of the work. I bought and sold used term papers, too. There were orders from Boston University, Northeastern, Tufts, Harvard and even Providence.

I also started a copy service. In fact, I got so involved in the business, I would have my own term papers done by my own company. I paid myself three bucks a page. It's like kissing your own ass. I was making three hundred bucks a week. I moved out of the dorm and set up a pad on Brattle Street.

There was a guy who lived next door who had ten reels of pornographic 8mm film. I told him I had college contracts and could rent the films to fraternities for ten a night. I told him I'd split fifty-fifty. I rented the films for fifteen a week, pocketed ten, and gave him five.

The money allowed me to live in a manner to which I was thoroughly unaccustomed. And I enjoyed every minute of it. I bought a white Porsche. My apartment was high-class. I had three walls lined with books by Kant, Hume, Spinoza, Shakespeare, Borges, Babel, Brecht – nothing but the best. I had one of the best collections of records in Cambridge. I specialized in Baroque. I loved Vivaldi, Bach and Handel. At night I drank red wine poured from a fine crystal decanter.

Although I liked the way I was living, the in-thing was to act poor. There was a run on identifying with the masses. Girls whose fathers made a hundred thousand a year would buy old clothes and five hundred dollar stereo sets. Phony Socialists. Do-gooding Cliffies would work a week in Harlem and then spend their winter vacation in Palm Beach or Spain.

I could play the game too. Not only did I have a Porsche, I also bought a broken-down milk truck. I grew a beard and wore work clothes. I bought a pair of mountain climbing boots and a sleeping bag. Frankly, I'd rather sleep in a giant brass bed with my head between two tits, than in a smelly bag in the woods. I never used the sleeping bag. But I let my friends know I had one.

Business was good, I was a B+ philosophy major, I had a pad and lots of friends. The only thing that was missing was super-girl.

Wally Jones was the biggest stud in Cambridge. He occasionally would fix me up with a slut or a hooker. I never was a piker when it came to broads. You only live once (not even that). I wouldn't think twice about spending fifty bucks on a broad who would stiffen my pecker. There is an old Hungarian proverb: "When the dick goes up, the brains enter the ass." It's the law of the lever. So what? If I have to be a shmuck over something, it might as well be a woman.

Anyhow, one night Wally Jones invited me over to his pad for a party. And there she was in all her Waspy magnificence: Kathy Weston. She was a candle in the darkness. The room lit up. Was it her long beautiful blond hair? Was it her face of peaches and cream? Was it her tits like two luscious honeydews? Was it her lovely legs that I envisioned straddled round my head? Who knows. But one thing I did know. This was true love if there ever was true love.

I knew that I had to play it cool with her. If I'd come on too strong I'd blow it. I asked Wally Jones what the story was on her. She was a sophomore English major at Radcliffe and the daughter of Sir Halifax Weston of Darien, Connecticut, Paris and Palm Beach. Her father was a frozen seafood magnate who also invested in land, mines and railroads. Sir Halifax Weston was one of the richest men in the country. Wally also told me that she was very bright and friendly. He gave me an intro.

"Hey, Kathy, how would you like to come for a ride in my milk truck?" I said.

"What kind of line is that, freshman?"

"Who says I'm a freshman?"

"Only a freshman would say something so shmucky."

"Well, I may be a freshman but I'm twenty-five, kid."

"I don't care if you're eighty, you can say something better."

"OK, would you like to come for a ride in my milk truck and I'll recite *Sailing to Byzantium* and *Leda and the Swan* by heart?"

"Better, but my answer to that is, buzz off."

"OK, how about this? Would you like to go for a ride in my milk truck over to my pad, where I'll play with your titties, grab your box, fuck you, eat you and give you a grilled cheese sandwich and cup of espresso coffee?"

"Now you're talking, freshman. Let's split."

Ah! I knew she was a girl with sensitivity. We hurried quickly to my pad, jumped into bed, and joyously frolicked in the sheets for a day and night.

I saw a lot of Kathy after that. We'd go to plays at the Loeb, the Proposition, the Boston Symphony. We'd go for rides on my sailboat on the Charles, picnics in the country, walks in the Common. It was a beautiful affair of culture, music and sex. She was a girl of many talents. And I loved her as much as I loved my own soul.

I went with Kathy most of that spring. Things started to get serious. She began to talk about the future. I told her that I intended to go to law school after my B.A. She was including herself in my plans. I wanted to marry her because I loved her dearly and I also wanted to get my hands on some of her old man's dough. But I was the son of Mendel the Bagel Baker, and it was absolutely forbidden to marry a shiksa.

I decided to take her to Brooklyn and ask my father's blessing. I already talked her into converting to the faith of my ancestors. We took the milk truck down to Flatbush to meet Poppa. On the way down I was a bit apologetic.

"Don't expect too much, Kathy. Remember, Pop is a poor widower with one eye who bakes bagels. He wouldn't cut the mustard in Darien."

"I love you, Harvey. Isn't that all that matters?" She was nice but naïve.

"Kathy, you don't understand. He don't even like goyim who convert. 'Once a Goy, always a Goy' he always says."

"Well, I thought you were marrying me, not your father! If your damn religion is so important, maybe we're making a mistake."

"I'm sorry, hon," I said. "You're the most important thing in the world to me. But if I can appease the old man, why not? I'm the only thing he has left in the world, be a bit understanding."

I told Mendel that I was coming home for Sunday dinner with a girlfriend. In my house that meant a possible bride. I did not mention that she was a shiksa. There was no reason to piss off the old man before I had to. When we arrived at the house, he took one look at Kathy and knew. But he did not say anything. Mendel went all out. A turkey, homemade bread, kishke, stuffed cabbage, apple strudel. He put the whole shmear for his daughter-in-law to be.

"Vell, vat does ya fodder do fer a living, Kateh?" Pop was blunt. He was what is known as a Grobyan. He could be crude without trying. Kathy was sweet.

"My father is an investor, Mr. Gross."

"Is dat a gud bizness?" Mendel asked.

"He makes a living, Mr. Gross," Kathy answered.

"Everybody calls me Mendel, you can call me dat too."

"OK, Mendel."

"Did ya like der soppa? Ya know I'm a baker, I made da strudel mineself."

"It was delicious."

"I vant to tawk to mine son alone in der next room. Ya don't mind, It's der man to man stuff. Her is a book of family piktchurs ya may vanna look at."

Pop took me in the next room and gave me a clout on the ear.

"Vats dis mit a shiksa! Ya modda would toin ovah. Vats a madda, you crazy or sometin?"

"But, Pop, she'll convert."

"Vunce a Shiksa, alvays a Shiksa."

"Bullshit, Pop. King Solomon married a Goy. King David married one too. She's beautiful, smart and she's got ten million bucks and I love her. And I don't give a shit what you say. Not only that, Pop. On her twenty-first birthday you will get a hundred grand. I promise you a condominium in Miami Beach plus two hundred a week. And if you don't like it, you can screw yourself."

I could talk to Poppa that way. We had an understanding. He was a tough egg and so was I. In high school I was captain of the football team, and I could kick in the teeth of anyone in the neighborhood. Deep down I was a gentle soul, but I let no one make a shmuck out of me.

"Vell, Harvey, ya know, I really like her very much. Come to tink of it she's beaudyfool. A regular Queen Ester. And as rich too. I'm givin you my best vishes. Buy da vay, have ya been givin her a preveddin shtup?" Mendel asked slyly, while giving me a friendly brush with his fist on my chin. I just winked. We had an arm wrestle and walked into the kitchen.

"Harvey tells me you wanna get married. Vell dis vun of happiest moments of mine life." He grabbed Kathy and gave her an overly loving kiss. Then he took out a hot ring that he bought from Rubin the Goniff for twenty bucks. He told her it was a three hundred year old family heirloom that he brought from Poland. She was pleased with him, he was pleased with her. We left.

I took her for a tour of Brooklyn: Coney Island, Nathan's, The Brooklyn Museum, Canarsie, The Heights and Prospect Park. She was impressed. We drove slowly, arm in arm back to Cambridge. It took six hours, but who cared? For a moment time stood still.

Kathy kept her room at Radcliffe, but moved into my apartment in Cambridge. Sir Fairfax had no idea that his daughter was living off campus with a circumcised shmeckel. I had no desire to meet Sir Fairfax for a while, but a tragedy changed that. There was an emergency phone call to the dormitory. Doris Fishman, a friend of Kathy, told Sir Fairfax that his daughter went to the movies. Doris immediately called my place and told Kathy to phone her father. She did so, and promptly broke out in tears.

"Oh, NO!" she cried. She hung up, put her head on my shoulder and bawled like a baby.

"For God sake, Kathy, what happened?"

"My...my brother Biffy was…killed in Viet Nam," she said, then sobbed hysterically.

"Oh shit. I'm sorry." What else could I say?

"When someone dies, you never have to say you're sorry," she yelped.

"OK, I'm sorry I said 'I'm sorry'."

"Oh Harvey, what'll I do?"

"How did it happen?" I asked.

"He was shot in the back at Trang Thuc."

"In retreat?"

"No. Ambushed."

"Frickin' Commies."

I really felt bad about it. Young Biff Weston, a marine lieutenant, snuffed out in the prime of his youth. For what? Nothing. Killing live people, what kind of business is that? He shouldn't have enlisted in the first place. Well, it wasn't all that tragic: now the old man's dough would be split two ways instead of three. There was Teddy, her brother, but no other children. And yet, when she cried, I felt like crying too.

"Harvey, I want you to come to the funeral with me."

"Kath, I don't want to meet your family under these conditions."

"I don't want to go home without you. It's not so bad when you're with me."

"But I don't know your folks. I'll feel out of place...with my beard and all that. Your parents are kinda straight. I'm not much at funerals."

"Please—for me, Harvey. It won't be so bad. They lose a son and gain a son. They'll like you. I just don't want to go it alone." As she implored, she grabbed my pecker and stroked it gently and said, "Puhleez come." I could not refuse. I loved her dearly. I was on my way to a funeral.

The next Sunday I drove with Kathy to the Weston estate in Darien. Kathy sat in the car, looking out of the window in dazed silence. When we arrived at the Weston home, I was awestruck by its magnificence. We approached on a half-mile circular driveway lined with poplar trees. The house was a tall, stately mansion fronted with imposing white pillars. The place must have had fifty rooms. In back of the house were a stable, swimming pool, tennis courts and servants' quarters.

I could see myself as the owner welcoming guests. A pleasant thought. "A spot of tea for the mawster of the house." Yow, that would be just numby. A young chambermaid making my bed while Kathy is at the meeting of a garden club. All those thoughts were in my head as I gazed at the opulent scene.

We entered the house. Inside we met Sir Fairfax, Teddy and Mrs. Weston. All three were dressed in black. Sir Fairfax was a tall, handsome man with graying sideburns. His Florida tan clashed with his black suit. Mrs. Weston looked like a done-up French poodle. Her nose pointed upward and so did her manner. Teddy was just a friendly Dartmouth freshman, not too bright, but pleasant.

The family exchanged griefs and pleasantries. I felt like I did not belong. Kathy had told Sir Fairfax that we were engaged. Surprisingly enough, he seemed happy about it. I had some doubts about how he would take the news. I did not think he would approve of a bearded Mocky from Brooklyn whose father was a baker of bagels. Yet he was overly kind. Even apologetic.

"Harvey, I'm sorry we had to meet under such circumstances. Things like this happen and there is nothing anyone can do about it. Although my heart is half broken, I'm happy for you and Kathy," he said.

Winning over the old man was a coup. Perhaps it was because he was so 'ungeshtup' with money, that it didn't make a difference whether or not his daughter married someone with money or not. Or perhaps it was because he had just lost a son that he did not want to invest in two griefs. I wasn't sure of the reasons, but the whole family dug me. Then again, I'm a really nice guy.

We drove down in the family Rolls to a country Episcopal Church where a private service took place. Close members of the family were there plus a uniformed marine honor guard. Also present was Elizabeth Tsimes, the broken-hearted girlfriend of the formerly alive Biff Weston. Elizabeth, veiled, in black, in tears, was a beautiful sight in the country church. She was young enough to find someone else. For her, no great tragedy.

The preacher read from *Ecclesiastes*: "Vanity of the vanities," saith the Preacher, "all is vanity. …a time to be born, a time to die… God hath made everything good in its time…"

A nice sermon. We walked out of the church teary-eyed and high-tailed it to the family crypt. And here I saw the truth. All the dough in the world did Weston not a fuckin' bit of good. He could make a million dollar call to the bottom of the earth: "Dis Heah Suh Fearfax. Return mah boy foh a two million dollah stock option."

"Solly, dis Chinee Laundly at bottom of ocean. Foh two million dollah only get gold-starched shirt and dish of flied lice. Solly. KLIK!"

Yes, with all the dough, Biff was as dead as the smallest philistine in Stuttgart on the Neckar. It is written: "A living dog is better than a dead lion." But then again, if all is vanity, not making anything is also vanity. The dead are all the same, but there is a quality of difference in the living. Crypts and cemeteries is a quality of difference in the living. Crypts and cemeteries I don't like if they belong to a Rothschild or to a beggar. I saw two large beetles crawling on the floor of the crypt. Rich food for you Mr. Bugs. A dead rich guy and a dead poor guy are both not worth a shit. But some are the living dead because they have to struggle every day of their lives just to get by.

I saw my shmear this way: if I could make a lot of dough without busting my ass, fine, and if I would have to bust my ass to live, to hell with it.

I was glad to get away from the place of death. I rode back to Cambridge with Kathy that night. Why should I think of sad things? Here I was with a rich, beautiful girl—me, a Harvard student, in perfect health, with a three hundred per week racket and a song in my heart. So for the time being, fuck you, Mr. Death! And we stopped at Howard Johnson's for a coke and a burger.

Back in Cambridge things went well. I had Kerd Literary Service and the film business for income, school for intellect, and Kathy for pleasure. Everything was fine until some morality freak in one of the fraternity houses told a Miss Twiddle that dirty movies were being shown at school. Miss Twiddle called the police, and the frat house was busted. The social chairman of the frat was pressured by the cops. He told the cops that he got his films from Gross Flicks, Inc. The police arrested me and confiscated fifteen rolls of film.

But that was not the worst of it. The next day the *Globe* carried the story: HARVARD FRESHMAN ARRESTED AS DISTRIBUTOR OF FRATERNITY PORNOGRAPHY. *The Crimson* carried it too: GROSS GROSSES TWIDDLE.

And with my shitty luck Sir Fairfax got wind of the story and steamed up to Cambridge from Darien. Sir Fairfax first went to Kathy's dorm and found out that she was living with me. He really was fuming. He stormed into my apartment at Brattle Street. Unfortunately, Kathy was there wearing only a nightgown. He was furious.

"Kathy, what is the meaning of this, living here with this...PORNOGRAPHER? I want you to leave here immediately."

"Hold on now, Mr. Weston," I said, "let me explain."

"There is nothing to explain, I don't want my daughter living with a sex fiend. You just keep your filthy hands off my daughter."

"I haven't been convicted of anything."

"I read it all in the *Crimson*. All the loyal alumni subscribe. And the *Crimson* doesn't lie."

"Please, Father," Kathy said, "Harvey is in trouble. I'll stand by him because I love him and I'm not leaving."

"You'll do nothing of the kind. I absolutely forbid you to marry him."

"Whether you like it or not Daddy, we are getting married."

"OK, if that's the way you want it. You won't get a penny from me. Not one sou. If you marry this degenerate, the good name of Weston will go down in infamy."

"We really love each other and that's all that counts," Kathy said.

"Would you like a cup of coffee, Mr. Weston?" I asked.

"NO DAMN IT. This is your last chance. Are you coming?"

"NO!" she said.

Sir Fairfax Weston stormed out of the apartment. Kathy put her head on my shoulder and cried. I felt really sorry for her. First her brother dead, then my arrest, and now a fight with her father.

"Kathy," I said, "maybe you should go to your father. After all, I'm no bargain, and what's more, he'll cut you off without a sou. You love him, too. Go."

I actually didn't want her to go, but I felt like testing her with a little speech.

"Harvey, I really love you and that's all that counts."

"But what about all the money you will lose?"

"On my twenty-first birthday, I will inherit a million dollars—whatever Father does. And money doesn't count if you really are in love."

That being the case, she was still hot.

"Well if you really love me, prove it," I said. And I caressed her head and slowly pushed it downward between my knees and my navel. And I found out that she really loved me.

BY GOD SHE REALLY DID!

Alan Lazarowitz was the hottest lawyer in Cambridge. He also was a personal friend and a crook. I knew with an honest lawyer I wouldn't stand a chance in the world. They actually caught me red-handed. Pornography sale and distribution is a felony. Some of the kids in the fraternity were under eighteen. They also got me on selling to minors. I went down to Alan's office and put my cards on the table.

"I'd like to beat the whole rap, Alan. What can you do?"

"They got you red-handed Harvey. It'll be tough."

"What about the 'redeeming social value' angle?"

"Not a chance with those films. Maybe with others, but not with a flick with a chick fucking a horse and blowing an aardvark. Where the heck did you ever get such sick movies?"

"What about not knowing the law?"

"Ignorance is no excuse."

"You mean I'll be convicted?"

"Of course not. I promise you'll beat the rap."

"How?"

"Shmuck, the way I beat every rap, if I have to. We just pay everyone off."

"Pay off who?"

"Well, you start with me. The case will be thrown out on a technicality."

"What technicality?"

"On the technicality that I get three grand, the prosecutor gets four grand, and the judge gets five grand. For ten G's, you're off."

"You're sure you can do it?"

"With Hyman Geltfast as the judge, how can we miss?"

"You mean Geltfast the former head of the State Corruption Commission is on the take?"

"Sure, the only people on anti-crime commissions are criminals. They're the only experts."

"Well, I'll be a son-of-a-bitch. It's a deal, Alan. Except—I don't have ten grand. How about five?"

"Don't bullshit me, Harvey. I know how much you make. In fact, I'm doing you a favor. You must have fifteen thousand, and besides, I know you're going with a rich shiksa."

"But her father cut her off without a sou."

"Too bad, ten or forget it."

"Seven?"

"Ten, not a penny less."

"Nine."

"Sold. It's a deal."

Actually, I had twenty grand, but why should I tell that chaser Lazarowitz?

The case came up a few weeks later and was thrown out just as Alan predicted. Kathy's father still would not talk to her. The following week I married Kathy. My father came up from Brooklyn for the small service. Alan, my friend, was the best man. Judge Geltfast performed the ceremony. He threw in the wedding for the same price. That's what I call a deal.

After we were married we took a larger apartment in Cambridge. We could not go on a honeymoon because it was near the end of the semester. We decided that we would travel around the United States all summer. We would camp in the Rockies, go to San Francisco. Kathy had friends at Stanford. Then we'd take a slow trip back to Cambridge by way of Canada.

Summer came and we made our trip. I dare say that was the best summer of my life. Kathy was kind and sweet. After every time we'd make love she'd kiss me on the cheek and say, "You're the greatest!" And I was.

After the summer we returned to school. I was a sophomore and Kathy a junior. Our life was beautiful. Occasionally I'd cheat on Kathy a little, not with evil intent. It is written: "What one doesn't know, doesn't happen."

I remember what Joe Agusta used to tell me: "A woman is only a woman, but a good cigar is a fuck." I asked him what it meant. He said it means, "Have a good time because you'll die someday." Joe sure knew where it was at. Anyhow, I never did anything to hurt Kathy. Our life was ideal until the terrible tragedy.

Kathy was an avid ping pong player. It was OK with me. Everyone has to have some kind of vice. She would play on Sundays with Mary Vaytug, a sexy woman, also from Radcliffe. One Sunday in midst of a heated game, Mary slammed the ball with all her might. Awestruck, Kathy opened her mouth. The ball slammed into her mouth, knocked her down and CHOKED HER TO DEATH!! Can you beat that, by a fuckin' ping pong game. I couldn't believe it. Mary Vaytug was in a state of shock and I was hysterical. Can you believe that, a living beautiful girl with everything in the world going for her, snuffed out? Pfft—like nothing. At least if she would have died swimming or by something noble. A shitty ball ended the life of the one I loved. I asked the attending physician for the ball. I crushed it and threw it in the river. Not only did I lose a beautiful wife, but it also was a million bucks going underground.

Since Mary Vaytug was in a state of shock I went to console her in the hospital. I tried to soothe her.

"You couldn't help it Mary, it was an accident."

"Oh no, I'm a murderer, I'm so sorry!" and she broke into tears.

"If you really kill someone, you never have to say you're sorry."

"Oh Harvey, I'm sorry, so sorry," she cried.

"You don't have to repeat yourself, all is fair in sports. It's only a game."

"But she's dead, Harvey. Dead!"

"I know and there is nothing we can do. Forget it."

"But I did it."

"Don't fret kiddo, because that's the way the ball bounces." I cringed realizing what I had said.

I notified Sir Fairfax and he immediately came up to Cambridge. He cried.

"Forgive me Harvey," he said with feeling.

"Sure, no hard feelings."

"If only I hadn't been such a fool."

"Don't worry about it Mr. Weston, she still loved you." I wanted to cheer up the old guy, after all he lost two kids in a short period of time.

"Two children dead, and so young, my own flesh," he spluttered.

"Well, you still got a son left. You know what they say, 'three strikes and you're out.' You're still in there pitching."

He left slightly consoled. It was too bad that we only met under negative conditions. He did not seem like a bad sort of guy. Sir Fairfax wanted Kathy buried in the family crypt. That was OK with me. I didn't want to go through another funeral scene but I had to. I wept like a baby at the funeral. I left Darien, never to return again.

After the funeral I went to Miami Beach to see my father Mendel. He, of course, knew of the death of Kathy.

He was sitting in an air-conditioned room of the fancy apartment I had set him up in, slightly drunk.

"Vell, dats, too bad aboud Ketty, she vas sutch a nize goil. Und vat ken ya do? Dats da vay da Matsa breaks."

"Pop, not only am I out a girl I love. We're out a million bucks."

"Dun't vury. Luv, Shmuv, es lung as ya got yer helt. Ya a kollitch boy a livin ye'll make."

"But I really loved her, Pop."

"Ach, vuts da difference, ya gud lookin boytchik. Op in Redklif, deer iz oder goils. Dee iz an old saying, 'Deer iz plenny oder gefiltes where dat fish came fum.'"

And the old Mendel, my one-eyed father, tapped me on the cheek tenderly with his fist.

I laughed.

My Literary Heritage

WHEN I WAS TWENTY MY MOTHER TOLD ME we had a second cousin, Nathan Bienstock, who was a writer. I was very impressed. At that time I was a fan of Brecht and longed to be an artist. To have writers in my family would be a literary heritage, a distinct advantage.

I asked my mother why Bienstock never came to the house.

"I don't know, I just lost contact," Ma said. "He was here once, but didn't come back. He used to hang around the cafeteria on East Broadway near the Forward Building. He was a little crazy, like all writers."

"Did he ever write a book?" I asked.

"He once wrote a book of poetry in Yiddish."

"Can I get a copy of it?"

"Why? You don't read Yiddish. Ya can't make a living from poetry. Do your homework."

"I'd like to meet him."

"You got nothin' to talk with him. He's an old man. Whyn't you do your homework?"

I was a sophomore at City College. My parents wanted me to be an accountant, but in high school I flunked math. I can't do a simple percentage. Numbers don't have faces; they can't sing or dance like the well-placed word. I was more interested in things that wear hats and making love to undressed women. Damn fractions!

I occasionally took the F train to The Museum of Modern Art. Every time I passed the East Broadway Station, I was tempted to get off and look for Bienstock, but I was shy and felt I wouldn't know what to say.

One day, I got up the courage and got off at East Broadway. I walked over to the Forward Building, looked around, and then went to the cafeteria on the corner. I bought a cup of coffee and a prune Danish and leafed through *The Village Voice.* Old Jews drank tea from glasses and sucked lemons. A man with a twisted nose and hanging jowls loudly slurped the bones of a whitefish tail. Was one of the old men in the cafeteria Bienstock? Reluctantly, I went to the counterman and asked if he knew Bienstock. He pointed to a old gent sitting alone in the corner. I walked up and saw a man in a shabby gray suit. The white hair on his head flowed in all directions. Around his neck was an old-fashioned green tie; the collar of his dirty, white shirt was slightly frayed. He had the air of someone trying to maintain a sense of dignity without the cash to back it up.

"Are you Nathan Bienstock?" I asked.

"Yeah, and who are you?"

"I'm Mendy Rosen, Frieda's son."

"Frieda's son. How did you know I was here?"

"My mother told me you were here. I was passing, and I thought I'd say hello."

"Sit down and have a cup of coffee." I sat. "Frieda's son? Well, that's nice. How is everyone at home?"

"OK."

"And you go to school?"

"Yeah, I go to City. I'm studying accounting."

"That's good."

"Well, actually I was thinking of becoming a writer. Mom told me that's what you did. I thought maybe you could tell me something about it."

"Ah, so you want to be a writer. What do you want to write about?"

"People, I guess."

"What about people?"

"I guess I'll write about their suffering and needs."

"Why do you want to do that?"

"Because I feel I should."

"And what will you do with what you write?"

"Sell it, if I can."

"Good. And what did you write so far?"

"Poems. They're not right yet," I said apologetically.

"Do you think you're gonna make a living from writing?"

"Why not?"

"Poems?"

"Yeah."

"Ya wanna talk about suffering?"

"I guess so."

"Hmm…Ahh…," Bienstock said as he tapped his fingers on the table. "Do you wanna work for a newspaper?"

"No. I'm interested in literature, not commercial stuff."

"Oh, a newspaper isn't fancy enough."

"It's not a matter of fancy. I want to be an artist, not a journalist."

"Then why are you studying accounting?"

"I gotta get by, for the time being."

"That's right. Send some stuff out. If they take it, good, if not, also good."

"I thought maybe you could tell me how to get something done. Like how to get an agent or a publisher." I was greener than the greenest grass. But a beginner must ask, or how else will he learn?

"Agents? Publishers? Ha. That's a laugh. Send 'em out to a magazine."

"Could you look at some of my stuff?"

"I don't know if I can help. I don't know English too good, especially if it is written by a college boy. Send 'em out. If they take it, good, otherwise, the hell with 'em."

"How did you get started?" I asked, hoping to learn some deep secrets of the writer's craft. Secrets that, I found in later years, did not exist.

"Me? I never got started. I was born in a small town in Russia. I came here at twelve and then I went to work in a shop. I sold some articles to the Forvits when I was around twenty. I wrote some poems, but I hardly made a penny. No Yiddish makes anything. We write from love-the only reason for anything. My worker songs were good, but nothing came of it. Rosenfeld was lucky. A Harvard professor, Leo Wiener, translated his stuff to English, and he became a big shot.

"A book of my poems was published, but I made nothing. Not only have I made nothing, I never will. Writing is very hard. Maybe if I was interested in business, I'd be better off. I never had any money to get married. Now look, I'm an old man waiting to die."

God! How awful it was. Is this what I had to look forward to? Perhaps because he was a failure his life was so bleak. But I would be a success. If poems wouldn't work, I'd try stories, TV plays, sculpture, anything. I was young and strong and I could do a hundred push-ups, and wouldn't give in. I was at a loss for words. What could I tell him? I got up to leave.

"Too bad, ya gotta go," he said. "Do you take the F train?"

"Yeah."

"My house is on the way. We'll walk over and I'll give you a copy of my book, if you want."

We walked to an old tenement house and went up to Bienstock's third floor apartment. The place was a dump. The kitchen table was covered with papers covered with Yiddish scribbling. The floor was covered with dust. A broken bookcase overflowing with books leaned against the wall. There were about a hundred copies of the same book – Bienstock's book of poetry. He picked up a copy, and brushed the dust off with his sleeve. He caressed the book gently. A broad smile was on his face. He looked happy.

"This is my book. It's called *Krummer Menschen*, means crooked people. You don't know much Yiddish do you?"

"No I don't. I'm sorry."

"It's OK. English is more important, anyhow." Bienstock took out a quill pen and wrote on the inside cover of the book – *To my cousin Mendy, Good luck in your life as a writer, and as a person. Best Wishes, your cousin Nathan Bienstock.*

"Well, this book didn't sell too good, but I enjoy it and it gave some people pleasure. Every now and then, when I pick it up, I feel better. And if I sold a million copies or one, I'd still be an old man. If I had a family," he said, "maybe things would be better. But it's too late for that. Forget what I said in the cafeteria. Do what you want. Write!" He shook my hand with a firm grasp, smiled and said, "Goodbye." When I left Bienstock, never to see him again, I was overcome with remorse and joy.

If I persisted in my literary aspirations, I could wind up as a lonely old Danish-eater who hangs around a cafeteria. But I had a book that was important to Bienstock and to me. A book I couldn't read, a book I couldn't evaluate. In the long run what difference does it all make? But, for the time being, we must do what excites and thrills.

I felt suspended by a thin strand, hanging precariously onto a life that had the opportunity of becoming rich and overflowing, despite the agony of one's inevitable death.

I rode home in the dirty subway, clutching the incomprehensible volume. Spangled metaphors danced in my head. I knew the way home, and I felt from deep within, a clenched fist pounding against my heart.

A Conversation with Martinson

MARTINSON, THE BIOPHYSICIST, was in New York on a business trip. He was vice-president of a large biomedical engineering firm in southern California. He had gone a long way from the old neighborhood in Brownsville where we both grew up many years ago. We hadn't seen each other in ten years. I invited him for dinner. I was living in a dump on the Lower East Side, driving a cab and writing plays. I had not gone far in the forty-three years of my life. Ten miles. I just crossed over a bridge from Brooklyn to get to the big city. And on the other side of the bridge I was still poor, single and struggling.

Since Martinson was a big shot and an old friend, I bought a couple of prime steaks, a gallon of wine and an overflowing cherry cheesecake. I cleaned up the messy room and threw a white cloth on the peeling kitchen table. I lit some candles and stacked Vivaldi records on the old phonograph. I believed I had an elegant dump. Martinson arrived at seven. He looked great. His sideburns were graying just enough to give him a distinguished look. He wore a very expensive dark suit, vicuna overcoat, a custom-made shirt, diamond cuff-links and a Bronzini tie. His shoes must have cost more than sixty bucks. Classy people always wear first-rate shoes.

No doubt Martinson had made it big. I was happy for him. If someone makes it, it may as well be a friend. You never know when you'll need a few bucks.

We talked about the old neighborhood and the guys we grew up with. Most were successful. Lazerowitz was a lawyer in Denver, Siegel owned a construction company, Harris was a professor, Gordon owned a clothing store.

In fact, all were making it, except me. Martinson knew this, so his attack began.

"Teddy," he said, "you know, you're a smart guy and I hate to see you living like a bum. You could do better than this."

"I manage," I said.

"Managing isn't enough. Part-time cab driving has no future. You make enough just to exist. This playwriting is a lot of crap. Now don't get insulted. I'm talking like an old friend. I'm a guy who likes you. We grew up together. I'm not talking about quality. Even if what you write is great, so what? It's too hard being poor."

"Wadda ya mean poor? That's prime steak."

"How much do you make a week?"

"Seventy bucks, but I make it in two days."

"It's bupkis. Living alone in two rooms. You ain't gonna get to heaven. You're a smart guy. Tomorrow you'll turn around and be fifty, the next day sixty. Then you're in a box with nothing." I had to defend myself. "What do you do that's so good?"

"Please, no comparisons. I'm not telling you I'm more or less than you. I'm talking about what's good for you. As a matter of fact, I do things that are good for others, and I make dough for myself. My company is working on an electric ear-sensor that will improve the hearing of fifteen percent of the functionally deaf."

"So what, most of what you hear is not worth listening to. I write plays that tell the truth."

"Truth? Bullshit. Don't give me the artsy-craftsy line. Plays are lies. Stories are lies. Poems are lies. Only the real world is true. You are a lie. I never read fiction, only factual history books. I never buy a painting; photos are closer to the truth. I read the stock reports and the *Times*. Poets, they're just nuts. Art is a substitute for reality, in your case. You live in a dream world."

"Did you ever hear from Sylvia Kretschman? She is in California."

"Ah, Sylvia, what a pair of boobs."

"Hah! Are those boobs art or science?"

"Science. They're science, I know I played with them myself. They're real. Do you know what art is? FALSIES!"

"Marty, I like to write plays. Why are you noodling me about it? Do I tell you what to do?"

"Sure, write. Do it in your spare time. I can get you a job selling prosthetic devices for fifteen grand. At night, when you come home, you can write your ass off. You can do both. If you become Neil Simon on the side, good. Give me tickets. I'll go to the show."

"I don't want to be a salesman, and I don't want to be Neil Simon."

"What! He makes forty grand a week."

"Good luck to him."

"Don't give me the noble artist sheet. What's wrong with making a buck? If you feel guilty with your dough, give it to the poor. They'll spend it on pink Cadillacs."

"Did you ever look at a picture of Getty? He looks like he's gonna bust out crying. He gets less pleasure from his dough than I get from mine."

"That's not the point. Money is no guarantee of anything, except avoiding poverty. A regular job won't insure immortality, good health, or a line of broads at your door. It will just improve the probabilities."

"I got good books, music, hobbies, what else do I need?"

"A future, wife, kids, a pension. Teddy, you may wind up in one of those single room tenements with TB. What do you do all day? You don't write all the time."

"I think."

"Thinking! That's the worst thing. Thinking drives you mad. With so much free time you'll get off your wick."

"Did you ever hear from Doris Bloom?'

"OK, I'll change the subject. Doris Bloom? No."

"You used to like her."

"Yeah, I always used to dream of porking her. She was in my history class twice. I couldn't score. I still dream about her."

"Ha! What are you doing dreaming? You're a realist. Dreams are art, FAKE!"

"Can't help it. It happens when I'm asleep. It's like being an alcoholic. Just because you have to drink, doesn't make it good."

"Well, I'm stuck on writing. Can't help it."

"Dreck. Everybody has to dream. But writers are oddballs, naive kids with visions of glory – people who can't express themselves through normal channels."

"Martinson, for a noodge you're OK. I met Barbara Harrison last week. She has a daughter who is a college senior."

"God! Like it was yesterday, when we were little kids. Now she has a daughter in college. Soon, Kaput, dead, finished...like she never existed, see what I mean?"

"Marty, Let me waste my life in peace."

"When was the last time you sold a play."

"Eh...Well I haven't sold any yet."

"Well, if you haven't sold anything in twenty years, what makes you think the next twenty will be different?"

"You never know what will happen in the future. You gotta do what you feel. If I don't sell anything that's OK too."

"A part-time cab driver don't even get a pension."

"I'll get Social Security."

"Won't be enough."

"I'll go on welfare."

"Putz, you went to college to go on welfare? Become a school teacher."

"I don't like to teach."

"So bang your head against the wall."

"Who me? I'm not complaining, you are."

"You just can't see the handwriting on the wall. But when you're poor, old and broke you can still come to me for a handout. You know why? Because I never forget an old friend." Martinson now dropped the lecture and went on to talk about the old days, when we were kids in Brooklyn. We talked late into the night about women, politics, philosophy and assorted nonsense. The wine fogged my brain enough to bring about the kind of euphoria that is not followed by a headache. An ideal high. At three, Martinson got up to leave. He invited me to his place in California. He was OK. I'm not like my socialist friends who constantly pick on those who make a lot of dough. After all Martinson was helping people hear better. And if he has a pool, good for him. Someone's gotta swim.

As I sat alone in the room after he left, I grew depressed. Perhaps Martinson's bleak forecasts were true. But even if Martinson were right, I would still head in the same direction. Perhaps out of madness or inspiration, or maybe just out of plain stupidity.

I like my work. I never was in the materialistic bag. I haven't asked much out of life, all I ever wanted was to be immortal and clean.

Dognose Rubin

RUBIN WAS A THIRTY-FIVE YEAR OLD GRADUATE STUDENT in philosophy at Boston University. He was a veteran of the Vietnam War, and used the GI bill to pay for his bachelor's degree. After he graduated, he worked as a substitute teacher of history. The students were out of control; he was climbing the walls, so he quit teaching and drove a cab. A Ph.D. would be a ticket to a better life.

When he'd get his degree, he planned to teach in a small Vermont College as a vest-wearing, pipe-smoking, burgundy-wine drinking professor. He would have a wife, two bright children, a house in the country. He would hold seminars in his living room on Aristotelian ethics, by a roaring fire, surrounded by adoring students—preferably young women. But he was running an "F" in Professor Casey's course Analytic Philosophy, and the dream looked like it was going down the tubes.

To add to his problems, Rubin was born with the most finely-tuned senses. He cold hear a radio playing in a whisper, almost a block away, and sniff cabbage cooking in a house as he passed it on the street.

Rubin once said to my friend Harvey Klein, "You had asparagus for supper last night."

"How the hell did you know that?" Harvey asked.

Rubin answered, "I have the nose of a dog." The name stuck. Everyone called him Dognose. Of course, he was a bit better off than Dennis Meckler who was nicknamed The Plague.

You may think that having finely-tuned senses are a blessing. After all, by your senses you know that you are alive. But in many ways, finely-tuned senses are a great curse. The ear that can hear the subtleties of the sublime movements of a Bach suite is greatly offended by snifflers and gum-crackers on buses. If you have a high-fidelity recording, each scratch of defect is amplified. If you can smell a dozen roses in the apartment next door, your nose picks up the odor from the toilet at the end of the hall.

But it was mainly the sounds he didn't want to hear that drove him up the walls. Once when he was on a crowded bus, on a rainy night, someone wearing earphones sat down next to him. He was playing some awful rock music that leaked into Rubin's ears. He thought he would go crazy. He got off the bus at the next stop and walked five blocks in the rain to his house. Dognose said, paraphrasing Mencken: "It's the little things that make life unbearable: a pebble in the shoe, a fly in the spaghetti, a woman's smile."

In addition to having super sharp senses, Dognose was burdened with another problem: he was a very shy person. His lack of assertiveness worsened the problems of super sensitivity. The neighbor's dog barked constantly; Dognose was too shy to complain. If he bought a bottle of milk and it was sour, he would not return it. If he got up enough courage to ask someone out on a date and he was turned down, he wouldn't have the nerve to ask again.

Klein, also a graduate student in philosophy, was just the opposite of Dognose. He plunged into life without apprehension. If a dog bit him, he would bite it back. He had the numbers of almost all the women at Boston University, and lists from Wellesley and Radcliffe. If ten women turned him down in one night, he wouldn't be shy about calling the eleventh. As a result, he had a date every Saturday night, while his friend Dognose would be home perusing his copy of the *Tractatus* of Wittgenstein and reading dog-eared copies of *Playboy*.

Once when Klein was in a bar with Dognose, a number of drunken students were making a lot of noise at an adjoining table. Dognose, of course, wouldn't ask anyone to pipe down. Klein put two beer cans in each of his huge hands, walked over to the noisy table, and said to the biggest guy, "If you don't quiet down, this may be your head." Then he slowly crushed the cans in each hand into little balls. The noisy students left.

"Harvey, you've got balls," Dognose said, "But one of these days someone may break your head."

"I'll worry about that if it happens, and it won't," Harvey said, "meanwhile you should be worrying about flunking out. What the hell has gotten into you?"

"There's something driving me up a wall. I can't concentrate on foolosophy. When I was living on Mass Avenue, the neighbor's German Shepherd's barking drove me nuts. I tuned into the dog noise and I thought I'd go off my wick. Each bark was a knife in my heart. I had to move, so Larry found me the apartment in Somerville. Next door there's pigeons. They coo early in the morning and late at night. They land on my windowsill, *coo! coo! coo!* It's like Chinese water torture. When I'm tense, I can't think. I just moved a few months ago and I don't want to move again. Sometimes I stay in my office 'til midnight."

"My good Dognose, you are too uptight. I recommend more mellowness. Adversity's sweet milk is philosophy. You should read the Stoics, preferably the school of Zeno. I also suggest the Manual of Epictetus, that preaches indifference to the woes of the world. Remember, nothing is intrinsically evil— there is only *you* and *your* judgments of events. *Your jug is broken; who the fuck said it wouldn't be? You have a bad father; who said you would have a good father (you were guaranteed only a father)*—that's right out of Epictetus, spiced up of course. I also suggest that you take up weightlifting and jogging. Run every night 'til you're ready to collapse. Go home, take a hot shower. You'll sleep like a baby. You won't hear a pigeon, dog, or wolf. And another thing—you need a woman. After all, why be annoyed by animals when you can be annoyed by a genuine human being? Who knows? You could even fall in love and make someone happy, and vice versa. Of course, a woman will probably make you a bit dumber. You know, all the great philosophers were bachelors—Schopenhauer, Kant, Hegel, Spinoza, Plato, Wittgenstein, Hume, and even Isaac Fig-Newton. But you don't have much of a career in philosophy, so you may as well not sleep alone."

"Bert Russell had three wives," Dognose said, "and he tried to make a move on anyone in a skirt—maybe even a Scotsman or two. So there goes your theory."

"No, my good Nose," Klein replied, "who said Russell was a great philosopher? I call him a mathematician. And who said I always tell the truth? I prefer to tell the truth only on Friday, in honor of Fria, the goddess of love. Today is Thursday. But, let's forget high-falutin' philosophy for a moment. I have a possible solution for your problem. Jane's best friend is Rebekah Klink. She's a senior studying animal psychology. Her specialty is owl eyes. She's studying the effects of light on owl eyes and how that determines the owl's behavior. People who know owls, know pigeons. If she doesn't know how to get rid of pigeons, no one does. Besides, she's single and not too bad to look at. Maybe you can kill two birds with one Klink."

Dognose called Klink. They arranged to meet in the animal psych lab. Rebekah was standing by a cage observing an owl. She wore a white lab coat. On her face were large circular glasses that contrasted with her tiny lips. In fact, she looked a bit like an owl. She wasn't bad looking, but she was nothing to get all bent out of shape about either.

Dognose sniffed his way around the lab, then told Rebekah that there was broccoli somewhere in the lab. Indeed, she had prepared a chicken and broccoli salad for lunch, sealed in a plastic container. He could sniff it out in spite of the overpowering odor of the owls. She was impressed with his talent, assuming from such sensitivity that he was a sensitive person. She had just broken a relationship with Curt Bristol, an accounting major whom she considered to be a boor. But he was occasionally nicer to her, and she didn't want to be alone.

Dognose told Rebekah about his problem with the pigeons. She responded, "There are a lot of possible solutions. Pigeons don't like noise. A set of wind chimes on the windows could be a first step. Next you can put some substance on the windowsills that pigeons don't like. There's a commercial product called Tanglefoot. Vaseline is cheaper. Put that on the sills, it may help. Screens or storm windows will keep pigeons from perching, too. A fake owl in the window can function the way a scarecrow does. Sometimes a fake snake will do the trick. The scare owl should be moved every few days; if it never moves, the pigeons will get wise. If there's a nesting place somewhere in the house, it could be closed off."

Klein was right. This woman knew her birds. Although he was troubled by the pains he endured from critters and insects—barking dogs, cooing pigeons, buzzing flies, stinging bees—he was deeply interested in knowing more about the animal kingdom. After all, there is a difference between wanting to know about the mating habits of lions, and having one in your living room.

They spoke with each other for five hours. They were clearly attracted to each other, the honey bee to the nectar. She told him all about her sad life. She came from a dysfunctional family in Quincy. Her father was a barber who was unemployed half the year. Her mother was in a nut house, and she had a brother she never spoke to. With the money she made in the lab and a part-time job in a restaurant, she just managed to get by. Since breaking up with Curt, she was seeing a shrink every two weeks.

People with such backgrounds are prime candidates for majoring in psychology. If one's problems come with heavy intellectual pretensions, the major is philosophy—at least that's what Klein told me.

Dognose saw that Rebekah was a woman from whom he could learn a thing or two, and perhaps teach. She was a twenty-two year old kid who never went more than 200 miles from Quincy. He'd traveled the world and read everyone from Aristotle through Zeno. Klein once told him, "Dognose, you should be involved with humans. If not, you'll hear your heartbeat. Never be alone. From those who know, learn. Those who don't know, teach. With those whose knowledge is equal, discuss and argue." With Rebekah there could be give and take. He invited her over for dinner, asking her to bring some anti-pigeon paraphernalia.

II.

Rebekah went to Rubin's apartment a few days later. She laid out her snake and fake owl. The sills were coated with Vaseline. Rebekah found a hole under one of the eaves where there were pigeon eggs. "Ah, that's where they nest. We'll close this off. This should solve the problem."

"What if it doesn't work?" Dognose asked.

"Then we'll try something else."

"What if something else doesn't work?"

"What if your grandmother had a beard? She'd be your grandfather. Why worry about all these hypothetical situations? Number one, it will work. Number two, let's have the dinner you promised me. By the way, what if the eggplant parmigiana is poisoned and we both drop dead? And what if the undertakers go on strike and we both have to lie here dead? Are you speculating that far into the future?"

"Ok, ok, you've made your point. I pretested the eggplant. It's safe. I can't guarantee the wine. Live dangerously."

They ate, they talked, they joked, they kissed. He did not make love to her that night. He did not have a sense of how far he should go. He went to bed dreaming he was making passionate love to her. He did not hear the pigeons that night.

He called Rebekah a few days later to tell her that he thought the problem was solved. But he had tuned in to a dripping faucet and could not get a good night's sleep. He invited Rebekah to a movie. The Rocky Horror Picture Show had been playing in Central Square for months. Neither of them had seen it. They enjoyed the movie very much. But it wasn't a complete success for Dognose, because someone was loudly chewing popcorn a few seats away. After the movie they went to Rubin's apartment. They talked, drank, kissed. But this time they made love. She stayed the night. Then there were morning glories—that's the term Rebekah used for sex in the morning. It was an appropriate word. The Latin name for the morning glory is convolvulus, meaning to roll together. Isn't that what they did? And wasn't it the morning? And wasn't it glorious?

They went out together for a month. Many nights she stayed over in the apartment. Then he asked her to move in. She did. She was living in a dormitory and didn't have too many possessions: a few suitcases of clothes, an old stereo, textbooks on animal behavior, psychology, anthropology. She did not read books other than what was related to her course work. Her records were just the kind of music Dognose hated. But he had to take her the way she was. After all, he had enough quirks of his own.

For the first few weeks she lived with him, things went well.

Then she suggested getting a dog. Rubin said absolutely no. Even though he was shy about saying no, he could not bear to have a dog in the house. Dogs made his life miserable. Then Rebekah suggested a cat. This did not appeal to him either. But at least cats don't bark. She did him a favor by getting rid of the pigeons. He was in love with her. What the hell, ok have a cat. Rebekah got an Angora cat from one of her friends. The cat's name was Wembly. He didn't like the cat, or the cat's name.

"What kind of name is Wembly for a cat?" he asked.

"That's the name Nancy gave him. I can't change it," she said.

"Well, the name makes me nervous."

"If a name makes you nervous, you need a shrink. I suggest that if you go to one, don't go to Harriet Ashley. She's my shrink."

"Ok, let it be Wembly." Dognose conceded on the cat, but many other things began to bother him. He would get very nervous when Rebekah would have long conversations on the telephone with her friends. He was reluctant to tell her to shorten them. Even when the conversations were low, he could hear them. She also snored a bit. This didn't bother him in the beginning, but it now seemed that the volume was increasing. When he kissed her he could taste the tobacco. Although she stopped smoking months ago, a residue lingered. When he was completely infatuated the tobacco did not matter, but now he could feel its pungency.

Rebekah was not his only problem. Professor Casey told him that he would definitely flunk analytic philosophy. He would lose his fellowship. He dreaded the idea of having to take a shit job in a store or, heaven forbid, work as a substitute teacher. To add to all the woes, he developed lower back pains. He imagined it was the onset of a fatal illness. He went to the university clinic and they couldn't find anything wrong. It seemed that everyone he spoke to had a lower back problem. If they didn't, they at least had a friend, cousin or uncle who had a bad back.

Someone tried to comfort him by saying he wasn't the only one with back trouble. It was no consolation that the problem was universal. After all, everyone dies. Does that make you feel better?

III.

As the semester was drawing to a close, Dognose saw his case as hopeless. Rebekah developed a bad cold. She was home in bed. She had the sniffles. Dognose could not bear the sound of sniffles. It was a sound that he abhorred more than most others. Temperament determines the offensiveness of a sound. It was not loudness that offended him, but tone. He could take the crescendo of a bass drum or clashing cymbals, but the scouring of a pan with steel wool would be unbearable. Schopenhauer, in his essay "On Noise," said that the most unbearable sound was the cracking of a whip. To each his own. Fortunately there were very few horses in Boston, and Dognose did not have to contend with hoof beats and whip cracks.

One morning at breakfast, while Rebekah still had the sniffles, she asked Dognose how he was doing in class.

"Rebekah, it's hopeless. I haven't figured out what I'm gonna do. But I can kiss goodbye being a philosophy professor. A C grade doesn't even count in graduate school, and with an F, forget it. I won't get another fellowship, and I'll never get into another program."

"Well, there are hundreds of other things you can do. You don't have to teach. I have the fellowship in primate study at Emory starting next year. You can come to Atlanta and get a job in something."

"No thanks. I can't take hot weather."

He buried his head in a newspaper. She looked at a textbook. She sniffled a bit. He could hear her crunch her toast. Just then Wembly hopped onto the kitchen table and stepped into a square of cream cheese. In a fit of anger, Dognose grabbed Wembly by the neck and flung the petrified cat off the table.

'Why don't you take your God damn cat, and get the hell out of here! Go back to where you came from!" he shrieked.

Rebekah was horror stricken. It was as if he had grabbed her by the neck and thrown her out. She was hurt to the core. He immediately regretted what he'd done. This was not the way he behaved. He was a shy cauldron ready to explode, and when he did, he hurt the one who was closest to him. He meekly said, "I'm sorry, I didn't mean it." It was too late.

There were tears in her eyes. “I didn’t know that you could be so cruel, not only to me but to a helpless animal. Ok. I’ll be out tomorrow. I thought that we could be good for each other, but you don’t know how to live with people or even animals. There’s nothing more to say.”

The next day she left and moved in with her friend Nancy. Rubin’s grief was boundless. He loved her, she was lonely, a lost soul. He had cast her out. He could have given some joy, but he had no talent in the art of comforting. Now he needed a friend. The only one left to give him a kind word was Klein.

IV.

Dognose met Klein two days later, at The Blue Parrot, in Cambridge. Klein had already heard the whole story from Jane, Rebekah’s friend. “Nose, I got the whole story from Jane. They’re best friends. They tell each other everything. You really screwed things up. Since I was the matchmaker, I kind of feel a bit responsible.”

“What can I say, Harvey? I regret what I did from the bottom of my heart. Will you ever forgive me?”

“Me forgive you, Dognose? How can I forgive, if I don’t blame? You’re my pal. You have to forgive yourself. Rebekah will get over it. She’ll go to Atlanta, get a Ph.D., meet another guy, perhaps someone better than you. Spinoza said that you must love yourself. I can’t do that for you. Now my good Nose, you have no girlfriend, no job, no future, and a bad back. According to my good friend Dante, at 35 you’re halfway to death. It’s downhill from now on.”

“Klein, you’re always good at cheering someone up.”

“Don’t despair, Nose. Remember what my good friend Yeats said, *We must laugh, we must sing, we are blessed by everything, everything is blessed.* Be good to yourself—it’s a moral imperative. Then maybe you’ll be good to someone else. My good friend Nietzsche said, *We have art in order not to die of the truth.* Now, you don’t want to die of the truth, do you? I suggest that you try some aesthetic occupation instead of your usual anaesthetic nonsense. In your case, stone carving would be good. You could literally get your rocks off. You should try to supplement your income by working as a baker of bread. Now what advice could be more specific than that?"

"Harvey, how do I know if I have rocks talent? I also don't think carving is a promising field. And I can't forget what I did to Rebekah."

"Nose, I'm a friend, not a magician. If carving doesn't work out, maybe you can play the viola. How the hell do I know what's best for you? But there is something that you could do well. Do it. My friend the Oracle at Delphi was asked what is the easiest and most difficult thing to do. The easiest is to give advice, the most difficult is to know thyself. What I'm doing is easy. What you have to do is difficult. But don't be too uptight over your fine senses. The banquet to sensibility is temporary. A time will come when the dogs will bark and you won't hear them; the pigeons will coo and you won't notice them; the worms will crawl and you won't mind them.

Now I suggest that we have a few drinks. As my good friend Alexander Pope said, 'Shallow drafts intoxicate the brain, but drinking largely sobers us again.' Of course, Pope was speaking of drinking in knowledge, but tonight I prefer wine."

Dognose and Klein schmoozed until The Parrot closed. They went to an all-night diner and carried on with their banter until daylight. Klein told me that Dognose took off and moved to Montana. He got a letter from Dognose saying that everything was almost under control. Rubin was working in a sporting goods store and living with an Indian woman. She had a dog that was driving him up a wall. The sounds of the coyotes interfered with his sleep.

Klein eventually lost touch with Rubin, or at least I think he did. Anyhow, I stopped asking questions about Dognose. After all, I have lower back pain myself, also arthritis, so I can't get too deeply involved in the problems of others.

The Man Who Only Read Jews

LEON KATZ, WITH HIS USELESS BA IN PHILOSOPHY, was tired of driving a cab. He took a civil service test and got a job as an employment interviewer. New York City is so big that everything is specialized. In a small town one would interview workers in all occupations. But in New York they would only work with a specific trade or skill. There were people who interviewed waiters, laundry workers, garment center workers, machinists, or "professionals," whatever that means.

In New York there are districts that specialize in only one thing: a flower district, a toy district, a jewelry neighborhood, a garment area, a theater district, an art gallery street. There are places that only sell store fixtures or electric motors.

In a city of specialization, Katz was not too surprised to find a man who specialized only in Jews. Well, perhaps a little surprised, for Harry Meckler wouldn't read a novel, short story, poem or play if it wasn't written by someone who was Jewish, or had some tenuous connection to something Jewish.

When Katz started working at the employment service, Harry was already there five years. Harry was about forty years old, he had two kids and lived in a three bedroom apartment in Queens. Harry immediately became a close friend of Leon. They ate lunch together daily. On Leon's first day on the job, Harry saw him reading *Doctor Zhivago.*

"You're reading Pasternak? He's Jewish, you know," Harry said.

"What difference does that make?"

"All the difference in the world. You don't want to read Goyim."

Leon thought that Meckler was joking and let it pass. In fact, Katz technically was not Jewish. His father was an atheistic socialist. His mother was of Italian Catholic ancestry, and he had no interest in any religion. Leon's father had a passion for left-wing politics until he found out that Stalin was a "son-of-a-bitch." Although old man Katz wasn't religious, he told Leon, "Sonny boy, deny nothing. Lenin is still a Ulynov, Stalin is still a Dzhugashvili, and Trotsky is still a Bronstein, and you and me are still Yids whether we like it or not. So if you have to be a Yid, don't be ashamed of it."

Daily Meckler would come with a book or information on the Jew of the day. "Leon, you should read *Miss Lonelyhearts* by Nathaniel West (used to be Weinstein). Did you know Marcel Marceau is Jewish? Douglas Fairbanks, the real name was Ullman. Victor Borge, you know the family name was Rosenfeld. By the way, you should read the plays of Harold Pinter, Arnold Wesker, Fernc Molnar, Arthur Miller. I'll bet that you didn't know Molnar was Jewish." For Meckler, converts were still kosher. Certainly Heine was on the "in list." So was Proust whose Jewishness was, to say the least, questionable. Montaigne, whose ancestry on his mother's side was Sephardic, was OK. Meckler was not joking about only reading Jews; that's all he read.

One day at lunch Meckler said, "You should read *The Death of a Bachelor* by Schnitzler. Also Joseph Roth's *Job* is a masterpiece."

"Harry, granted these guys are good, but haven't you heard of Shakespeare, Dante, Moliere, Hemingway, Joyce, Fitzgerald, Faulkner, Goethe, Homer? They ain't chopped liver. Why don't you read them?"

"I read them in college. They're OK. Life's too short. I'm a religious man. Everything worth reading is in the *Torah* and the commentaries. I read secular books because I'm fond of literature. It's a hobby. You can spend your whole life just studying Maimonides. You couldn't understand the whole *Talmud* if you studied it for a thousand years. Where will I find time to read Homer? And I owe it to my people to read their books. I could even specialize in Italian Jews: Primo Levi, Carlo Levi, Umberto Saba, Natalia Ginzburg, Alberto Moravia. Moravia's real name was Pincherle. Did you know that?"

Leon knew that suggesting any non-Jew would be a waste of time. If he told Harry to see a play by Eugene O'Neil, Harry would say, "Why should I when I can see a play by Arthur Miller?" When Leon suggested *War and Peace*, Harry's response was, "Too long, bad for the eyes." However, there were books that they both read: Malamud, Roth, Bellow. There was enough to talk about over lunch.

After Harry knew Leon for a few months, he said, "You must come to my house on Friday night for a Sabbath meal. My wife is a great cook. I'll show you my library. It's probably the best private collection in Queens."

II.

It was a Friday in June. The Sabbath starts at sunset. Harry left to get home before dark. Orthodox Jews don't take the subway on the Sabbath. Harry had to get home before dark. Leon had a few hours to kill. He went to a peep show on Eighth Avenue, browsed in a bookstore, stopped at a kosher bakery for an apple pie, and took the F train to Forest Hills in Queens.

On the apartment doorpost was a mezuzah in a wooden case, a piece of parchment inscribed with texts from Deuteronomy, as commanded in biblical passages. Inside there were mezuzahs on every door. Candles were already lit. There was a challah bread on the table that was set for a feast. Harry introduced Leon to his wife, Sheila, and his twin sons who were fourteen.

They stood around the table. Harry gave Leon a skullcap. Harry and the boys, of course, were wearing skullcaps too. Harry chanted, in Hebrew, the blessing over the wine. Then they sat down. Next he cut the challah and said the blessing over the bread.

Sheila was a pleasant, good looking woman, a bit on the plump side. The two kids were well behaved but didn't say much.

"Harry tells me that he has lunch with you every day. He's happy that you're working with him."

"Lunch is the best part of the job, but coming home to a good dinner is even better," Harry said. "A man wouldn't bake an apricot strudel, but Sheila does. The only problem is that good wives make fat husbands."

"You're not fat," Leon said.

"That's because I have self-control, but every man needs a good woman. Sheila, don't you know anyone where you teach who would be good for Leon?"

"We just hired a third grade teacher, Barbara Greenstein. She's thirty-two, time to be married. I'll give you her number, she's very nice." Leon wondered if this fix-up wasn't pre-planned. He was uneasy about arranged dates. Barbara Greenstein probably was Orthodox, and he wasn't even Jewish according to Orthodox law. They believe your mother has to be Jewish, or you must convert to be a member of the tribe. He didn't fit the bill, although he felt Jewish. He was reluctant to say, "I'm not really Jewish." He didn't want to hurt Harry's feelings. And what difference did it make?

"Thanks for the offer, Sheila, but I'm already seeing someone." That was a lie, but it would put an end to the matchmaking.

"Leon, you son-of-a-gun, why didn't you tell me? We will all get together sometime and go out."

"Yeah, sometime."

"By the way, is she Jewish?"

"Of course."

The meal proceeded with Matzo ball soup, stuffed chicken, potato kugel, mashed carrots, salads, and ended with Sheila's apricot strudel. After dinner Harry gave out books to chant the grace. The books were in Hebrew. Leon couldn't read them. Harry and the kids chanted along, and Leon sat smiling.

"Now that dinner is over, I will show you the piece de resistance: my library." Harry had a three bedroom apartment—one for him and Sheila, one for the kids, and the other, the largest, was the library. Henry opened the door slowly.

From floor to ceiling on all four walls, it was filled with bookcases. In the center of the room, an island of bookcases up to the ceiling. A desk stood in the corner, piled with books. "You should see the cellar, Leon. I have three bins filled with books. There are over five hundred books in the living room, and it's not even a library. Along this wall I keep the holy books in Hebrew and the commentaries; then I have a Yiddish section here. I have some science books, biographies, histories, fiction, plays. You name it, I got it."

Harry had books from Hannah Arendt and Danny Abse to Israel Zangwill and Stefan Zweig. The science books included Stephen Jay Gould, Isaac Asimov, Carl Sagan. Biographies of Einstein, Bohr

(Jewish mother), Enrico Fermi (Jewish wife), Richard Feynman. Biographies of musicians: Bernstein, Mahler, Mendelsohn, Schoenberg, Berlin.

"Harry do you have any book without a Jewish connection?"

'Maybe one. I have *Webster's Third International Dictionary.* His first name was Noah. Who knows?"

III.

About three weeks after the dinner at Meckler's, Leon went up to Mona's on West 94th Street. Mona's was a hooker joint frequented by guys with moderate incomes. Not high class call girls who charge a few hundred bucks a pop, but not the low class twenty dollar street walkers, where you're liable to get a dose of clap or something worse. Mona's was a fifty dollar house. It was clean and relatively safe. Leon usually saw the same girl, Rosie. He always used a rubber, and would feel pretty good after a session. Now he thought that he hadn't lied when he told Sheila he was "seeing" someone. He was seeing someone, but that was surely not what Sheila had in mind. For all he know, Rosie could have been Jewish too, but religion was not a topic of discussion at Mona's.

When Leon exited Rosie's room, he saw Harry leaving an adjoining room. Harry's face turned as red as a fire engine when he spotted Leon. "Harry, you won't read Hemingway, but you'll "read" a Goyishe hooker," Leon joked. "Do me a favor, forget that you saw me here," Harry said as he ran out without saying another word. Leon regretted what he said in a thoughtless moment, but what is said is difficult to unsay.

IV.

The next day, in the office, Harry kept his distance. Leon said he was sorry about the joke and suggested that they have lunch. Harry said he was busy. They greeted each other but that was about it. The daily lunch stopped. Occasionally Leon would try to strike up a conversation.

"How's Sheila?"

"OK."

"The kids?"

"They're fine."

"Read any good books lately?"

"A few."

"What books?"

"Can't think of any now."

After a few weeks of giving Leon the cold shoulder treatment, Harry was depressed. He had no one to talk to about books, and he lost his lunch partner. He was a mentor, Leon was his protégé. He was a teacher without a pupil. There were hundreds of books to suggest, but he couldn't talk books to MacDonald or Morelli, and Rabinowitz was practically an illiterate who just read comic books. He liked Leon very much, but he was ashamed of what he had done. No, not that ashamed of what he did, but ashamed of being seen.

Another week passed. Harry could no longer resist. "I've totally forgotten what happened a few weeks ago. A secret we keep until they bury us. Let's be friends so we can talk. OK?"

"OK. Friends," Leon said.

"Let's have lunch tomorrow."

"Yeah, let's have lunch."

The spell was broken. The next day Harry came with a couple of tuna fish sandwiches and Sheila's homemade potato salad. "I'm treating you to a lunch made by my wife. We'll eat it in the employee cafeteria. By the way, have you read *Crowds and Power* by Elias Canetti? He won the Nobel Prize. He's Jewish you know."

Mona Levy

THE DIRECTORS OF THE LOUVRE WERE GOING CRAZY after the discovery of a secret diary by Leonardo da Vinci, found during the restoration of the Palazzo Medici-Riccardi.

The writing was authenticated to be in the hand of Leonardo. It began with these unsettling words:

While working on The Battle of Anghiari *in Florence, I was visited by a Jew and juggler from Mainz called Moritz Finkelboim. He claimed to be an admirer of my work, and brought me a gift. It was a painting, in my style, of a woman with an odd smile. He called it Mona Levy. When he left my house he was killed by a wild horse. He was carrying a sack with a copy of the* Old Testament *in Hebrew, a prayer shawl, and two small black boxes with leather straps that may have some magical religious purpose. Since he left no forwarding address when he died, he was buried in an unmarked grave in Florence. I studied the Mona Levy and discovered that it was a good painting—good, but not great. In honor of Finkelboim, I displayed it as one of my own, with a slight adjustment in the title.*

The four Directors a the Board meeting were Chairman Jacques Couteau, Marcel Fourchette, Jean Cuiller and Gaston Geldzhaler. "Gentlemen," Cuiller said, "this is a disaster. The honor of France is at stake. For over five hundred years the Mona Lisa has been a Leonardo. It's the chief attraction in our museum. It's probably the most famous painting in the world. Not only that, David Hockney recently wrote a book claiming that the painting was done by using lenses projecting an image on a wall. He makes a pretty strong argument that the painting was traced! Now the public will think that we are morons."

Forchette, the noted collector and anti-Semite, piped in. "Will people come to see a Finkelboim? Who the hell is he? Why is it that the Yids always have to throw in their three centimes. I just hope that Leonardo was joking. You know he always told jokes."

Forchette's remarks angered Geldzhaler, the only Jew on the Board. "I strongly resent the remarks about us Yids. Finkelboim didn't cause this problem, Leonardo did. So what if a Fink painted it? A painting is a painting. Is it any less if it's a Finkelboim?"

Couteau chimed in. "If it is a Finkelboim, it is less. Everything is in a context. There is the Leonardo oeuvre. We can relate the painting to the High Renaissance. We know who Leonardo knew. He was a student of Verrocchio. He can be placed. A Finkelboim is a nobody. There aren't great painters who only have one work, and nothing is known about him, except that he was killed by a horse."

Forchette couldn't be stopped. "Dreyfus the traitor was a Yid. Benny Levy the Maoist was a Yid. Danny the Red was a Yid."

"Oh, Shut up!" Couteau yelled. "Let's not get into a race war where we'll never accomplish anything. I suggest that we take a week off to come up with a plan. All the newspapers know about the diary. The phones have been ringing off the hook. The comment to the press, Gentlemen, is 'no comment.' Until we know what to say, we say nothing. I told the Minister of Culture that unless there is a complete study of the matter the painting is still a Leonardo. I've referred all questions from the media to him. Let it be on his head. The meeting is dismissed until Wednesday at noon. Monsieur Geldzahler I want you to stay on. I have to talk to you privately." The others left. "Gaston, I need a favor. I happen to know that you are a distant cousin of Lustiger, the Cardinal of Paris. He is the only cardinal in the world who's a Jew. As you know, he claims to be Catholic by faith, but still part of the Jewish people. When he was hidden by Christians during the war, he adopted their faith, my faith, and became a good Christian. Being a bit pushy, like most Yids, no offense meant, he worked his way up to the top banana in France. I know that when Jews have a problem they go to a rabbi for an answer. I've heard that the Cardinal is knowledgeable about art. I want you to go to him. Pick his brains. What he says carries more weight than all the lackeys in the government combined. See him and come back with an answer. France is depending on you."

Couteau knew how to tweak Geldzahler, make him feel important, as if the whole Republic would fall if he would not visit the Cardinal. Of course, Gaston agreed.

Geldzahler was a non-believer, but a Jew, whether he liked it or not. At times, he was a defender of the faith. At other times, he was totally indifferent to the Jewish question. He was a Jew because his parents were. If he were raised as a Christian or a Moslem, he would have been that. To him one religion was as good — or bad — as another. Random acts determined his fate. Had his father stayed in Poland, he would have been toast. But just before the war, the old man moved to the south of France and opened a photography studio. Gaston was born in 1946. He lived in Paris all his life. But to a Forchette he would never be French and neither would any of his children or grandchildren.

Gaston's wife suggested that they move to Israel. "Go to Israel! It's out of the question. It would be like going from the frying pan into the fire. You want to know why not? I'll give you a list: I don't believe, I don't speak Hebrew, all my friends are here, the children are here, the political situation there is a disaster, I'm a respected art historian here, we do well, I love France, and they make better croissants in Paris than in Tel Aviv. Period. Case closed." That was enough for Mme. Geldzahler. They would not go to Israel. However, the Jewish problem intruded into his great love — art. Gaston was a student of what Professor Alcaly called the Jewish Emotionalist School of Paris: Soutine, Chagall, Pissaro, Modigliani and Pascin. They were good, but Leonardo was better. The Finkelboim case would ignite a wave of anti-Semitism. The whole thing was irrational, but who's rational these days?

II.

Geldzahler met the Cardinal, at Notre Dame Cathedral, on a bright November morning. He was ushered into an elegant office. Lustiger sat behind a huge Louis XIV desk. In his flowing red robe, he looked like the prince of the church that he was.

"Gaston, it's good to meet my cousin after all these years. Who could believe that two punk kids whose parents lived in the backwaters of Poland would be here, today, in Notre Dame. You, a famous art dealer, on the Board of the Louvre, and I, The Cardinal of Paris. It proves that there must be a God. No?"

"Your eminence, you know I'm not here to discuss theology. I've sent you the Finkelboim File. With all due respect, you didn't get to be a big cheese in the church by your good looks alone. Everyone knows that you're very smart. Something should be done about the Finkelboim matter now."

"Gaston, I'm a man of faith. To be an artist you must have faith too. To solve a problem one must believe. One does not need reasons. One believes. Aquinas gave proofs for the existence of God. That's not necessary. One knows God exists because he feels it here," Lustiger said, pointing to his heart.

"Sir, will you get to the point." Gaston regretted saying that. After all, he was talking to the Cardinal. But Lustiger took no offense. For a cardinal, he was quite mellow.

"OK, Gaston, here's the deal. I know the Mona Lisa like the back of my hand. I've studied it for years. The picture is a beautiful enigma. What is it? Blobs of paint on dumb canvas. But it conjures up a world. Now we have minimalist painters. They put almost nothing on canvas. That's good and bad. If nothing's there, you can insert everything. But a little bit of pigment directs your thoughts. My theory of art is: If it's this, it's not that. It is a theory I call Thisness. The idea is profound, think of it when you leave.

"The solution to the 'Finkelboim Affair' is simple. Have the picture hang just the way it is. After the name, Leonardo, place a question mark. After the mark place a sign in bold letters. **THERE WILL BE NO EXPLANATIONS.** Never explain. Now you have two mysteries for the price of one: the smile and the question mark. In the church we have, at least, three for one. Once the viewers become accustomed to the signs, they will incorporate it into the painting. For those who want to see a Leonardo, it will be a Leonardo. The Finkelboim crowd can believe whatever they want. The anti-Semites will never be pleased with whatever you do. Remember what Duke Ellington said: 'If it sounds good, it is good,' and if it looks good, it is good, and if it reads good, it is good. Now I have to go to a hearing about a priest who defaced a Picasso that he thought was obscene. A cardinal's job is never done. This audience is over. Go with God."

III.

Geldzahler went to the Board of Directors meeting on Wednesday and presented the Cardinal's recommendations. Forchette was not too happy that someone might still consider the painting to be a Finkelboim. But he was a good Catholic, and he could not oppose Cardinal Lustiger's suggestions.

Today, the Mona Lisa hangs in the Louvre with the question mark and **NO EXPLANATIONS** sign. Two months after the Board made the changes, when the museum was closed, Gaston stood before the Mona. He gazed at the enigmatic smile. In it he saw Dreyfus eating a ham sandwich, Moses splitting the Red Sea.

Acknowledgments

MANY OF THE TEACHERS AT UNIVERSITY OF MASSACHUSETTS AMHERST, Mount Holyoke College, SUNY Albany, and Smith College, were very helpful to me with my literary obsession. To name a few: James Ellis, Mount Holyoke College; Richard E. Kim, University of Massachusetts Amherst; Tamas Aczel, thesis advisor for the MFA; Denis Johnston, Smith College; Robert Tucker, editor of the *Massachusetts Review*; Jules Chametzky, University of Massachusetts Amherst; and Joseph Langland, University of Massachusetts Amherst.

Many years later I left the Amherst area. I was fortunate enough to be in classes sponsored by New York State Writers Institute with John Montague, Douglas Glover, Lydia Davis, James Lasdun, Robert Pinsky, and Leonard Michaels.

Some of my teachers and many of the students in these classes have become close friends. The list of names would take a few pages. Alas, I let many of my mentors down; I fizzed out like old seltzer.

My teachers have also been the books I've read by Samuel Beckett, Franz Kafka, James Joyce, Heinrich Heine, Itzik Manger, Johann Wolfgang von Goethe, Mary Oliver, Emily Dickinson, Paul Celan, A. E. Housman, Philip Larkin, Walt Whitman, William Butler Yeats, William Blake, Isaac Bloomstein, Robert Burns, Peter Heinegg. David Axelrod, and Barnett Zumoff.

Also, I should acknowledge the good friends who published my two books with their effort at their own cost, and I didn't ask them to do it. The first group was Despa Press, friends of mine who started the press to publish my book of plays, *The Ice Cream Parlor.* Alan Casline of Benevolent Bird Press published over 250 copies of my poetry collection, *Monkeyshines.* And thanks to Therese Broderick for all her kind help. Special thanks to Paul Amidon for being a superb editor.

No day goes by when I'm not looking for a lost object or lost name.

"Oh, lift me as a wave, a leaf, a cloud!
I fall upon the thorns of life! I bleed! "

(Percy Bysshe Shelley, "Ode to the West Wind")

Or better yet,

"We must laugh and we must sing,
We are blest by everything,
Everything we look upon is blest."

(William Butler Yeats, "A Dialogue of Self and Soul")